THE NOR'WESTER

OTHER BOOKS BY
DAVID STARR

Golden Goal (2017)

From Bombs to Books (2011)

The Nor'Wester

David Starr

RONSDALE PRESS

THE NOR'WESTER
Copyright © 2017 David Starr

RONSDALE PRESS
3350 West 21st Avenue, Vancouver, B.C., Canada V6S 1G7
www.ronsdalepress.com

Typesetting: Julie Cochrane, in Minion 12 pt on 16
Cover Design: Nancy de Brouwer, Massive Graphic Design
Maps: Veronica Hatch and Julie Cochrane
Paper: Ancient Forest Friendly "Silva" (FSC) — 100% post-consumer waste,
    totally chlorine-free and acid-free

Ronsdale Press wishes to thank the following for their support of its publishing
program: the Canada Council for the Arts, the Government of Canada through the
Canada Book Fund, the British Columbia Arts Council, and the Province of British
Columbia through the British Columbia Book Publishing Tax Credit program.

 Canada Council Conseil des arts
for the Arts   du Canada
 Canadä
 BRITISH COLUMBIA
ARTS COUNCIL
An agency of the Province of British Columbia

Library and Archives Canada Cataloguing in Publication

Starr, David, author
    The Nor'wester / David Starr.

Issued in print and electronic formats.
ISBN 978-1-55380-493-2 (softcover)
ISBN 978-1-55380-494-9 (ebook) / ISBN 978-1-55380-495-6 (pdf)

    1. North West Company--Juvenile fiction. 2. Fraser, Simon,
1776–1862 — Juvenile fiction. 3. Fraser River (B.C.) — Discovery and
exploration — Juvenile fiction. I. Title.

PS8637.T365N67 2017   jC813'.6   C2016-907436-6   C2016-907437-4

At Ronsdale Press we are committed to protecting the environment. To this end we
are working with Canopy and printers to phase out our use of paper produced from
ancient forests. This book is one step towards that goal.

Printed in Canada by Marquis Printing, Quebec

to the people of Fort St. James,
the Nak'azdli, and to those
who have lived on the banks of the
river since time immemorial

ACKNOWLEDGEMENTS

Thank you to Ronald and Veronica Hatch and Ronsdale Press for your editing, guidance and belief in this project. I am deeply in your debt. Thank you also to my wife Sharon and my family for your support. In particular I would like to thank my father who believed in Duncan Scott for a long time before this book was published. Finally, I would like to thank Cal Mackay and the Charles Best Secondary School Social Studies Department.

The British Isles

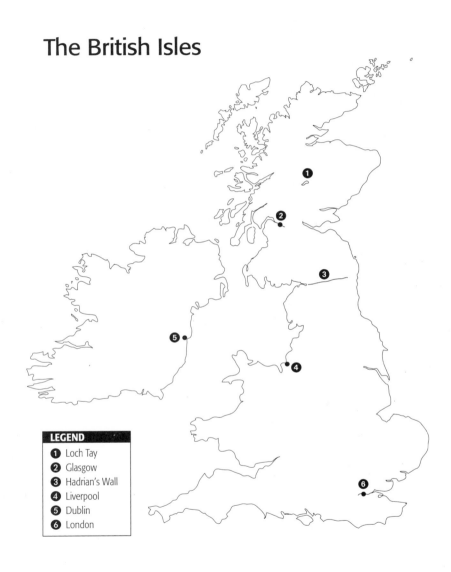

LEGEND
1. Loch Tay
2. Glasgow
3. Hadrian's Wall
4. Liverpool
5. Dublin
6. London

Route of the Nor'Westers
by Canoe and Portage

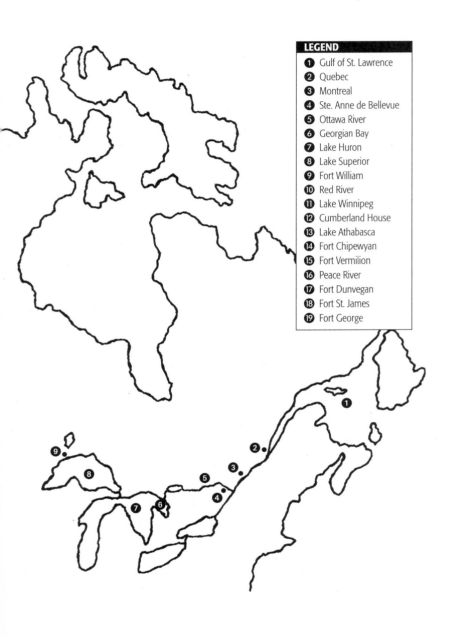

LEGEND
1. Gulf of St. Lawrence
2. Quebec
3. Montreal
4. Ste. Anne de Bellevue
5. Ottawa River
6. Georgian Bay
7. Lake Huron
8. Lake Superior
9. Fort William
10. Red River
11. Lake Winnipeg
12. Cumberland House
13. Lake Athabasca
14. Fort Chipewyan
15. Fort Vermilion
16. Peace River
17. Fort Dunvegan
18. Fort St. James
19. Fort George

Simon Fraser's Route to the Sea

Chapter 1

GLASGOW, 1806

I FEAR I WILL NEVER see the Highlands again. No more scent of hay and heather rising sweet on the summer air alongside my father. No birdsong filling my ears as I till the stone-scrabbled land, planting barley and wheat. These simple things of my old life, gone forever, missed with a fondness I never felt at the time.

Now? Naught but dust, the clatter of looms and the strands of cotton that rise above the mill floor, twisting like spider-webs. There are no wildflowers, no songs in the mill, just the cursing of angry foremen as they hit us, urging us to work harder, to clean the jammed machinery, to weave faster, to make money for the laird.

Fourteen hours a day we toil, my mother, father, sister and I. Fourteen hours of sweat and aching bones and back-breaking labour, on a machine as hungry for life and blood as it is for the cotton that comes on the ships from America.

I haven't lost any fingers yet. Or my life, unlike the lass who worked next to us. Her name was Emma. She was fifteen like me, from Aberdeen, a thin girl, tall, with green eyes and hair the colour of ripe summer corn.

It jammed, the loom she worked with her family, and she was sent to clean it. She reached into the works with her slender arm and as she did, the machine sprang to life. Her hand caught in a cog and she was lifted into the air, dragged screaming and writhing into the wheel.

She died in front of her family, crushed to death, begging for help that did not come. And when the foreman finally arrived? He pulled her wrecked, twisted body from the guts of the loom and fined her parents a day's wages for disrupting production.

A year has passed since I last saw the mist-shrouded flanks of the mountains that rise above the black waters of Loch Tay. A year since the men came with clubs and guns and letters of eviction. Our farm leased by my family for five generations, now too valuable for people, turned over to sheep.

Our old cottage is gone. Burned to the ground. Our cows? Shot by those smirking men who said the same fate would greet us if we ever returned to the Highlands. Now? We live in Glasgow, all four of us in a wee dingy room in a soot-stained brick tenement on the south bank of the River Clyde. Our water comes from a well on Caledonia Road instead of the stream that ran clean and clear beside our cottage. Our toilets? Clay pots, their stinking contents thrown out into the street when they are full. This is how we live, that is until this cold April morning when, shivering and weak from a fever, I struggle to get ready for work.

My father takes one look at me and shakes his head. "Nae. Stay home, lad. Ye'd do more harm than good, the state yer in. And yer sister will keep an eye on ye too; ye could both use the rest."

I mumble a farewell and go back to sleep, hardly feeling my father put an extra blanket on my body and my mother kiss me goodbye. I slumber until just past noon and would have slept longer still had my sister Libby not shaken me roughly awake.

"Duncan, get up. Something's happening, there's a commotion outside."

"What's going on?" I ask, shaking the cobwebs from my head.

"A dinnae ken. Something terribly exciting by the sounds of things. Let's go and see."

We slip down the narrow staircase to the street, and it's then I see the smoke. "The mill! It's burning to the ground!" yells a small boy. There are many cotton mills in Glasgow but the only one within a short distance of our house is Hamilton's Cotton Mill. Our mill.

I rush forward, a sense of dread rising in my stomach. I turn the corner and see the place engulfed in flames. Huge columns of thick, choking smoke fill the air, and handfuls of dazed, ash-covered workers who'd escaped the inferno gasp for breath on the street.

In full panic I speed towards the main gates. "Mother! Father!" I cry frantically as I search the crowd, but my parents are nowhere to be seen. Panic threatens to overwhelm me until Libby catches sight of Angus Drummond, a Highlander who works in the mill and lives in the room next to us.

"Angus! My parents?" I beg. "Where are they? Have ye seen them?"

"In there." The old man points a trembling finger towards the inferno. "A beam fell down across the door! They're trapped, lad! I tried to help but there's naught I could do."

"Nae!" I push my way through the crowd towards the fire, sheltering my face from the flames and the billowing black smoke. Libby catches up to me and holds tightly to my arm.

"Duncan! Stop! It's too dangerous!" I shake free of her grasp and stagger forward towards the gates, fighting the waves of heat that water my eyes and make me gag for every breath. More than twenty yards from the main gates I'm forced to stop, and then, with a realization that hits me like a fist, I know my parents will never escape the flames.

I collapse, weeping. Libby sits beside me as we watch help-lessly while the huge mill burns until nothing remains but a pile of ruined brick and charred timbers.

"Out of my way!" I lift my head to see a rider on a fine black horse quickly approaching. The horse whinnies to a stop in front of me, and a fat, toad-like man, looking ready to burst through his expensive clothes, climbs down from the saddle.

Cecil Hamilton, the rich English owner of what had once been the most profitable mill in Glasgow, waddles through the crowd, jowls bouncing, sweat glistening on his fat face as he swats at people with his ornate walking stick. "My mill!" he cries over and over in his strange English accent. "It's gone!"

I feel a sharp pain on my arm. Through tear-filled eyes I see Hamilton glaring angrily at me, his walking stick raised to strike again. "What the devil have you got to cry about?" he demands.

"My family was in there, my laird," I choke.

"Your family was useless Highland trash! They probably started the fire in the first place. They deserved to die. Now get out of my way!"

Before Libby can move, Hamilton strikes her hard across the back with his stick. My sister cries in pain and falls onto the blackened cobblestone street.

In a flash, my grief is replaced with blinding rage. I grab the walking stick from his fat hands and with a hard clean whack strike Sir Cecil Hamilton squarely across his head.

"Don't ye touch my sister!" I scream, landing blow after blow on the Englishman. Hamilton stumbles and falls to the ground, screaming for mercy, but I can't hear a word and stop only when the strong hand of Angus Drummond stays my arm.

"Nae! Duncan! Stop fer guidness sakes!" Angus pleads. In shock I drop the stick and stare blankly at the crumpled form lying still on the ground. "Ye nearly murdered him, lad! Ye'll hang fer this if ye're caught. Flee! Flee fer yer life!"

Chapter 2

WE RUN, THE SYMPATHETIC crowd parting as we pass. Many have lost family in the fire and few bear any love for the English mill owner. We race towards home and stumble up the steps to our room.

In the space of a few moments we've become both orphans and fugitives, and whether it's my fever or the sudden realization that my parents are dead, I reel, vainly fighting the urge to throw up.

From my knees I watch helplessly as Libby stuffs our few possessions into a small canvas sack. "Get up, Duncan. We need to leave now." In the corner of the room is a loose floorboard under which Father concealed our meagre savings. We weren't supposed to know about the money, but it's impossible to keep secrets in such a small place. Libby reaches under the board, tucks the bag into her coat and walks towards the door, listening nervously for the sound of pursuers. Frozen, I remain on the floor shaking, my eyes now riveted on a picture of our cottage in the Highlands my mother had embroidered years before.

"Take it," she says gently, lifting it from the wall and giving it to me. "'Tis all we have left of them now." Libby cautiously opens the door. There's nobody about and so, without a backward glance, we hurry down the staircase.

Remaining in Glasgow is now utterly impossible for me. People who steal a mere loaf of bread in Scotland are routinely jailed or transported overseas. To assault a man of Hamilton's stature in front of hundreds of witnesses? I'll be executed if I'm caught.

My sister pulls my coat tightly around my shoulders, places a worn cap upon my head, and we step out onto the street, alive with talk of the fire and the attack on Hamilton.

We walk swiftly and deliberately, keeping our faces down, hoping desperately we won't be recognized. I panic when we pass a troop of soldiers questioning a familiar, soot-covered man. By the looks of the blood and bruises on Angus's face, the troops have been rough on him.

"Oi! Come on then," says a soldier. "We know the boy's a mate of yours. You'd better tell us where we can find 'im." We turn our faces and walk quickly on, leaving Angus at the mercy of the soldiers. There's nothing we can do except pray our friend stays silent long enough to let us escape.

Numb with grief and still battling illness, I walk for hours beside Libby, hardly noticing when the bustle of Glasgow is replaced by the quiet of the Scottish countryside. The change is remarkable. Spring flowers bloom in the fields, songbirds chirp and flutter about the hedgerows, and for the first time in months, I smell the rich musty odour of freshly turned earth.

Tears spring from my eyes but Libby forces me to push the painful thoughts from my mind. "There'll be time enough for that when we're safe, brother. One foot in front of the other until we're far away from Glasgow. One foot in front of the other."

With as much speed as we can muster, we pass furtively through the rolling hills of the Scottish Lowlands, avoiding towns and people as much as possible. We sleep in barns and sheds when we can and under hedgerows or the open sky the rest of the time.

What little food we eat comes from the fields: half-rotten seed potatoes, turnips and carrots left over from the last harvest, washed down with cold water from the countless small streams that run down from the hills. It isn't much, but it keeps us alive.

Four days after fleeing Glasgow I ask the question that has been consuming me since the fire. "Libby, do ye think Mother

and Father would be alive if we'd gone to work? Could we
have saved them?" My guilt at their death has been growing
by the day.

"Nae. We'd have died as well, I reckon," she replies.

"Do ye think Hamilton's dead, too? Did I kill him?"

"A dinnae ken fer sure, Duncan, but I doubt it."

"It doesn't matter," I say flatly. "Dead or alive they won't
stop hunting until they find me."

The thought chills my sister and she quickens the pace.
"Then we'd best keep moving as far and as fast as we can,
even if that means going all the way to London."

On a cool rain-swept afternoon, a week after leaving Glasgow, we come across a tumbledown collection of old stones
stretching far across the countryside. I've never seen these
ruins before, but I know immediately what they are.

"In ancient days, the Romans conquered England," my
father had told me one day back at Loch Tay as we gathered
in hay. "They pushed north, vanquishing all who tried to re-
sist them, and it wasn't until they reached Scotland that they
were finally stopped. The Romans built a barricade to protect
themselves from us, and to this day Hadrian's Wall still stands
as a reminder of the strength of the Scottish people."

"Have ye ever seen the wall?" I'd asked, full of pride.

"Nae lad, though I'd love one day fer us to go together."

I pause for a moment and put my hand reverently on one
of the ancient stones, my grief overwhelming me. My father

will never see this wall. He will never see anything again.

"Hadrian's Wall is everything ye said it was, Father. I just wish ye were here with me."

I step through the ruins, and as the tumbledown stone wall passes out of view behind me, I take a deep breath, compose myself and press into England — and the unknown.

Chapter 3

THE AROMA OF COOKED meat lures us off the path, towards a campfire burning cheerfully next to a large chestnut tree. Beside the fire is a cart full of pots and pans and other assorted metal goods. A horse is tethered nearby, nibbling contentedly on fresh green shoots of spring grass.

A cauldron hangs over the fire. Something delicious bubbles in the pot, and my mouth waters at the smell. We haven't eaten for a day now, not since we found an old cabbage left in a field, half rotten and full of worms.

I look around everywhere but the cauldron's owner is nowhere to be seen. "Libby, I'm starving! Let's eat!" My eyes are fixed on a piece of meat floating on top of what seems to be a stew.

My sister shakes her head forcefully. "Nae Duncan! How would ye feel if someone stole yer food?" Ignoring the rumbling in my stomach, I reluctantly turn away from the pot.

"I'm impressed, boy," says a strange, high-pitched voice. "By the look on your face I'd have sworn you was gonna take me dinner."

Startled, I follow the voice to the base of the chestnut tree where, dressed in brown and almost perfectly camouflaged against the bark, sits the oddest man I've ever seen.

The fellow is tiny, hardly taller than a child, but he must be sixty years at the very least judging by his long grey beard. "What are your names?" he asks.

"Marie, Sir. My name is Marie Drummond and this is my brother Angus," Libby says cautiously, and I pray that our old friend won't mind the lie.

The little man stands up. "Well then, Marie and Angus Drummond. Name's Tinker. Now come and eat; you both look as if you're about to faint." The man dips a ladle into the cauldron and fills three metal bowls with its steaming contents. "Rabbit stew." He passes me a bowl of the most delicious-smelling food I've ever had. "Eat your fill and then tell me what two young Highlanders are doing alone in England, so very far from home."

"We were living in Glasgow, Sir," Libby says between mouthfuls. "There was a fire and our parents died. There was nothing left fer us in Scotland afterwards and so we left." I look worriedly at my sister but she adds nothing else.

"I'm sorry to hear that," the old man replies sympathetically, "and before Glasgow? Neither one of you strike me as city folk."

"Aye, 'tis true. We lived in the Highlands," my sister admits. As sad as it is, this part of our tale is safe enough to tell.

"Many have been forced off the land and into one of them cursed factories on this side of the border, too," Tinker says when Libby finishes the story. "So what are you going to do now? Walk aimlessly about England?"

"A dinnae ken!" I'm hit with a sudden touch of desperation. "We can't go back home, and if we don't get work soon we'll starve."

"Well, me young Highlanders," says Tinker, "I'll make you this offer. I'm on me way to Liverpool, ten days south of here. If you help me sell me wares along the way I'll feed you and give you a blanket. I'm a poor man and it ain't much but it's the best I can do. And who knows? Sometimes opportunities come along when you least expect them. What do you say?"

I look anxiously at Libby, and when she nods in approval, I shake the old man's hand happily. "In that case I say thank ye very much!"

Tinker sounds pleased. "Angus and Marie Drummond. It seems we're now partners! You'd best get some sleep. We'll be leaving at first light, and morning has a habit of sneaking up on you before you're ready for it."

It's wonderful to have a companion, and the days that follow are a blur. We help Tinker sell pots and sharpen the knives, scissors and scythes that housewives and farmers bring to the cart. In return we're fed and sheltered; we even earn a few pennies of our own. I like Tinker. He's kind and patient and, for the first time since our parents died, I feel safe.

The journey south is uneventful until a day's travel out of Liverpool when a sudden violent storm forces us off the road and into the shelter of a copse of trees. "I'd planned on travelling for a few hours yet," Tinker says, "but we'd best stop here. It looks like we're going to be in for some nasty weather. Set up the canvas, find us some dry wood and I'll make a fire for tea."

As we make camp, thunder cracks in the sky above and large raindrops splash onto our heads. More than just the bad weather weighs on me. "I'm worried, Tinker," I confide. "A dinnae ken what we're going to do next."

"Don't worry, lad," Tinker replies with a confidence I don't share. "I've a feeling something unexpected will happen to you soon."

Chapter 4

THE SHARP TANG of salt water fills my nose as we reach the edge of the city. "That's the Irish Sea you smell. Liverpool's one of the largest ports in England; you'll see strange things here from all over the world. Mind you keep your wits about you, though," Tinker warns. "There are plenty here who'd cut your purse or even your throat if they had the chance. People will do all sorts of bad things for a guinea or two."

Libby squeezes the small bag of coins hidden in her jacket and looks around fearfully, seeing robbers and murderers in every corner. She's not told Tinker about the money and has ordered me to do the same.

Tinker seems not to notice her discomfort as we travel

along the docks until we meet a large, tin-roofed warehouse. "I have to meet me business associate here on the docks," he says, walking to the open door. "Go for a stroll. I'm sure you'll find more interesting things on the waterfront than an old peddler replenishing his stock of pots and pans. But don't forget to keep your eyes open. Like I said, the docks ain't the safest place in Liverpool."

Dangerous or not, the waterfront is a remarkable place. The docks are lined with ships, a forest of masts in front of dozens of wooden and brick warehouses. Crates of all sizes litter the piers, and everywhere we look, men of all shapes and colours busily load and unload cargo from ships. One ship in particular catches my attention, and I shudder as massive rolls of cotton cloth disappear into its belly. I saw far too many of those rolls in the mill.

We also see people on the docks who are most definitely not sailors. Men, women and children my age, and younger, lounge against piles of cargo. They seem full of nervous expectation, and when I see the posters stuck onto the walls and pilings I thank my mother that over my father's objections she'd taught Libby and me to read in the long, wet Highland winters.

"*Come to New York,*" "*Boston*" and "*Halifax,*" the advertisements say, and though I've never heard of these places before, the words fill every fibre of my body with exhilaration. Wherever these cities are, they must be very far away from Glasgow and Sir Cecil Hamilton.

I see a boy a few years younger than myself sitting on a crate. "Where are ye going?" I ask, my voice trembling.

"Boston," the boy replies with a Highland lilt. He gestures at the *Leopard*, a small three-masted ship berthed at the end of the wharf. "Ma says in America there's land and food fer everybody and that we're gonna be rich."

His words hit me like a lightning bolt. "Libby, 'tis our chance! Let's go with them!"

"A dinnae ken, Duncan," she replies nervously.

This is not the response I'd been hoping for. "Why not? Would ye rather stay here with the soldiers chasing us?" I say sharply, not willing to let this opportunity slip by.

"Let's talk to Tinker and see what he has to say. Besides, passage isn't free. We have some money but I've no idea if it's enough."

Reluctantly I agree. We've wandered a great distance since leaving Tinker, and we take several wrong turns amongst the maze of ships and warehouses before we find our way back. Libby waits outside as I walk into the warehouse. Ahead I see two shadows, one quite large and wearing a hat, the other small and familiar. "Tinker!" I call. "We need to talk to ye."

Tinker takes several steps towards me while the other man fades into the darkness. "What is it, lad? We ain't quite done our business yet."

"I have something very important to ask ye about," I reply, anxious and excited.

"Wait outside for me by the cart and I'll join you presently," says Tinker before I can explain. With no other choice, I rejoin my sister and sit on the cart waiting impatiently as Libby scratches the pony's ears.

An old sailor sitting under a blanket against the side of the warehouse catches my eye. "Can thee spare a copper for a wounded veteran of His Majesty's Navy?" he says to Libby. "Name's John. I was on the *Captain* with Admiral Nelson at the battle of Cape St. Vincent. We gave the Spaniards a sound thrashing that day but I didn't escape unscathed."

John lifts the blanket and Libby gasps when we see both his legs have been amputated below his knees. "His Majesty's Navy has no use for a cripple, even a war hero, and I've been here on the docks ever since, begging kind lasses like thyself for a few coppers to buy bread."

Libby places a penny into John's outstretched hand. "Here ye go, ye poor man."

"Libby! We need all our money to sail to America!"

"A penny won't buy us passage, Duncan, but it will feed this man fer a day or two," admonishes my sister.

John places the coin inside his tattered coat. "God bless you, miss. Thy generosity won't be forgotten. But you, young man, could learn a thing or two about kindness. Someday thine own life might hang in the balance. When it does, I hope you meet people more charitable than thyself."

The sailor takes his leave and shuffles away on his stumps. "I bet he's going to spend that coin on drink," I mutter.

Libby is unperturbed. "And so what if he does? It was the

least we could do." Long experience has taught me there's no point arguing with my sister, so I ignore her. When the peddler finally steps outside the warehouse, I feel as if I'll burst.

"So what bee's gotten into your bonnet?" he asks.

"There's a ship on the docks taking people to Boston, and we want to sail on it."

"Boston." Tinker has a faraway look in his eyes. "Do you even know where Boston is, lad?"

"That way?" I say, pointing to the west.

"It is but you have to survive crossing the ocean to get there. Many ships leave this port and ain't never seen again. They just disappear, swallowed up whole by the storms. There are waves a hundred feet high out there, you know. Untold thousands have died on the Atlantic. There ain't nothing wrong with taking great risks, but know what you're getting yourself in for."

The old man stares at a seagull diving amongst the ships' masts. "A part of me would like to go as well. I thought about it once but I was never very brave, and I'm too old for such travels now. Ain't much use for anything really," he adds strangely, "not no more."

"Do ye have any idea how much it would cost to travel to Boston?" I ask.

"How much money do you have?" I look at Libby and she reluctantly shows the old man the sack we took from our old place in Glasgow. He peers inside and shakes his head. "Ain't enough by far. You'll both need to work for a year or two, but if you save your wages you can be on your way before you know it."

"A year?" I cry. "We have to wait a whole year?"

Tinker casts an eye back into the dark warehouse. "Why don't I go and talk to my friend about a job for you? They're always looking for strong backs on the waterfront. What do you think?"

"Thank ye, Tinker, that would be appreciated," says Libby.

"Wait here then," the peddler instructs. "I'll have a quick word and I'll be right back."

Impatient and upset, I sit on the back of the cart, waiting for the old man to reappear. Suddenly I notice a piece of paper sticking out from underneath Tinker's large whetstone. Out of curiosity I lift the stone to see what it says, and as I read, my guts churn and my head feels as if it's spinning like a top.

"Libby." My tone is quiet but my sister recognizes the terror in my voice and she hurries over. Hand shaking, I hold up the paper. It's a poster. A poster with the date, my name and a very recognizable drawing of my face.

"*Wanted for Attempted Murder,*" it reads. "*Sixteen-year-old Duncan Scott, Recently of Glasgow. Five-guinea reward if alive, three guineas dead. The fugitive is believed to have entered England in April 1806, likely in the company of his sister Elizabeth Scott.*"

Chapter 5

"HOW COULD HE have known about —" My sentence is cut short when Libby clamps her hand tightly over my mouth and pulls me behind a stack of crates. Eyes bright with fright, she points to the warehouse.

Tinker and a large man in an English army uniform emerge from the depths, with the soldier holding a copy of the wanted poster. "The boy told me his name was Angus, Major," Tinker says, "but that's definitely 'im."

Tinker clears his throat and holds out his hand expectantly. "The reward? Five guineas if captured alive, it said. I saw the poster in Carlisle a week ago, could have slit both their throats while they slept to collect the easy three, but I didn't. I'm kind, I am."

The major drops a gold coin into the peddler's hand. "You are a very compassionate man, indeed," he says in a tone that indicates otherwise. "There's one guinea now. You'll get the rest when my men have the boy in irons. Where is he?"

"Out here somewhere." Tinker scans the waterfront. "I told 'im to wait by the cart. Went for a walk probably. They don't suspect a thing — think I'm their friend."

A dozen armed soldiers march out of the warehouse and stand in the entryway, waiting for orders. "We'll find him," the major says. "That scum nearly killed a nobleman! He'll soon have his neck stretched for it."

Libby takes my hand, and the two of us creep slowly away from the crate and, after making sure we aren't seen, we turn and sprint down the dock. "How could Tinker do this to us?" I ask, my stomach heaving.

"Fer the money," Libby replies bitterly. "Now let's find that ship."

"But we don't have enough money! We need to pay for passage, remember?"

"And ye believe Tinker after what he tried to do?" says Libby as we speed towards the *Leopard*. "He'd have said anything to stop us from leaving so he could collect the reward."

My hopes soar. Libby's right. We could have more than enough money for passage. With a bit of luck we'll soon be on the ocean, free and far away from Cecil Hamilton, the soldiers and Tinker's treachery.

We round the corner to the *Leopard*'s berth and the world comes crashing down around me. The *Leopard* has sailed.

The ship is only one hundred yards out of port, but it may as well have been in America already.

A loud commotion rises behind us. "In the name of King George, get out of our way!" cries a soldier. Both of us panic. Then I see that another ship, the *Sylph*, is tied up alongside the dock, only a short distance away. The gangplank is extended and unguarded, like an arm beckoning us aboard.

Libby sees it as well. "Duncan! Get on that ship and hide! I'll wait here and distract them! It's not me they're after, and if yer caught ye'll die!"

"Libby! Come with me! The soldiers are almost here!"

"Are ye mad? If I do, they'll climb on board, tear this ship apart and find the both of us." Libby grabs my hand and drags me to the gangplank. "No matter what happens, stay hidden until they go. I'll be fine. They'll probably just ask some questions, then let me go. I'll get ye when it's safe. Just don't move until I come. Promise me ye won't."

"I can't leave ye!" The thought of being taken from my only family is like a dagger in my heart.

But Libby is insistent. "Get on that ship this instant, Duncan!"

"They must be down here!" a soldier yells. "We 'ave 'em now!"

I reluctantly step onto the gangplank. "I love ye, Libby."

She thrusts the bag of coins into my hands. "I love ye too, Duncan. Just promise me ye'll stay hidden no matter what."

"I will," I vow, speeding up the gangplank. I'd never been

on a ship before, and I scan the vessel quickly, looking frantically for a safe place to hide.

I try several hatches but discover they're locked. What to do? Then I see a small boat sitting on the deck, covered in canvas. In desperation I lift the tarp, crawl into the bow, and bury myself under a pile of musty-smelling sails.

"There's the girl!" a soldier cries as the sound of boots quickens along the wooden dock. "You! Missy! Where's your brother?"

"On that ship," Libby says defiantly as my heart sinks. Has my own sister betrayed me too?

"Damnation! He's 'alf a mile out to sea!" Then in a flash I understand what my sister was thinking. We may not have been able to sail on the *Leopard*, but the ship can still help us as a decoy. I feel the faintest flicker of hope. We may just get out of this after all.

"Shall we get the Navy?" a soldier asks.

"Don't be daft. The Royal Navy won't mobilize for a mere boy, no matter who he beat 'alf to death!"

"So you think your brother has escaped justice do you, young lady?" Even through the canvas, I recognize the voice of the major who gave Tinker the gold.

"Defending yer family is not a crime, Sir," Libby says, trying her best to be brave.

"It is when the man he attacks is a friend of the King. Search the other vessel," the major orders. "This could be some sort of a trick."

Several sets of boots clamber up the gangplank. "Waste of time, this," a soldier mutters. "The brat's a league out to sea, laughing at us. A bit of a coward though, don't you think? To abandon his sister like that? What sort of villain could he be?"

"A terrible coward," agrees the other. "You're probably right. He's on the other ship, no doubt, but you know the army same as me; do as you're told or else. Let's 'ave a quick look and get this over with."

"You there!" a voice cries. "What are you doing on my ship?"

"Searching for a wanted criminal. What's it to you?"

"I'm the captain of this vessel," comes the curt reply. "People boarding my ship need my permission, even soldiers of the realm."

"Sorry, Sir," the chastened soldier says, deferring to rank. "Orders. We're looking for a terrible criminal who fled the King's justice."

"King's justice? The wretch probably stole a carrot from some duke's kitchen."

"Oh no, Sir! I ain't sure exactly what he's done but there's a five-guinea reward on his head. Murdered a lord or something by the sounds of it."

The captain relents. "In that case be quick about it. We sail on the next tide and you two don't look like the type who'd fancy a trip across the Atlantic this time of year."

I hear the men rattling hatches and checking doors.

"Everything's locked up tight," one says. "Let's just 'ave a look in that small boat over there so we can tell the major we did our jobs proper."

The soldiers approach, boots thumping on the deck of the ship, and I will myself to stay as still as possible as they near, stopping mere inches from my head. I hear the canvas cover pulled open, hold my breath and freeze. One movement, one slight cough and I'm done for. I wait for what seems to be an eternity. Then I hear the boots walk away.

"He ain't aboard, Sir," one of the soldiers reports as the men walk down the gangplank. "The brat must be on the other ship — just like the girl said."

"I told ye," Libby says. "Now ye can let me go and be on yer way."

"Oh, I don't think so, lass," the major replies. "You're coming with us."

"But I haven't done anything wrong!"

Hidden safely in the lifeboat I fight the rising horror in my chest. This is not part of the plan at all! The soldier was right: I am a coward! The urge to jump out of the little boat and save Libby almost overwhelms me until I remember my promise. *Don't move until I come to get ye.*

"Wanted or not, you can explain things to Colonel Phillips yourself, young lady," the major says. "He'll be most displeased with this turn of events and will want to hear about it from you personally. Someone has to pay for your brother's crimes, and it seems that person is you."

Chapter 6

I WAKE WITH A START. I don't remember falling asleep and for one brief second don't even know where I am. Slowly I peel back the canvas covering and squint in the bright sunlight — to receive the shock of my life. My sister, the soldiers that took her and the entire port of Liverpool have vanished.

All alone, the *Sylph* bobs on the swells, ropes and timbers creaking gently on the waves, seabirds wheeling and soaring in the blue afternoon sky. Before me stretches the English coast: cliffs and beaches, fields and towns spreading out as far as I can see.

But I've no time to process the scene. A pair of strong hands pulls me out of the boat and tosses me down hard onto the rough deck of the ship. "Stowaway!" someone yells.

I look up and see a compact man in his mid-fifties with a short cropped white beard and intense green eyes studying me. "It looks like there was someone hiding on my ship after all."

"Throw him overboard, Cap'n!"

"Nae, Tom, we're not criminals but if I'm to believe the dockside scuttlebutt, this boy is. And he must have done something quite terrible; five guineas is an awful lot of money for the life of one so young."

The sailor called Tom is a hulking bear of a man with thick black curly hair and large muscles. His scowling face and the wicked-looking knife grasped in his hand leave no doubt at all what he'd do to me if given the chance.

"A stowaway and a felon? Sir! We don't need his kind on board. Besides, we'll be jammed solid when we pick up the Irish! Please, Cap'n, let me and the boys take care of him!"

I don't like the idea of being "taken care of" by Tom or anyone else, and am terribly grateful the captain ignores the suggestion. At least for now.

The captain stares into my eyes. "Tell me your story and convince me not to take you back for the reward, lad. Don't lie to me. I'll smell it before it comes out of your mouth, and if I do, then Tom and the lads will have their way with you."

So this is how it ends: turned over to the army or tossed over the side of the ship into the waves. The truth won't make much difference anymore, so I start to speak. "I was born in

Loch Tay. I lived there my entire life until the men with guns arrived." For the next ten minutes I tell my story. When I finish I wait apprehensively.

The captain nods his head sympathetically. "My name is Isaiah Smith," he says. "My father was a collier. He was killed in a mine explosion when I was six. My mother died two years later, and I was sent to sea. I know what it's like to lose a family. I'll not turn you over to the army, even for fifty guineas."

"Cap'n! You can't let him stay on board!" protests Tom to the agreement of most of the other sailors.

The captain's reply is low but it carries the power of a gale. "This is my ship, and I'll thank you to mind your place, Tom Jenkins, and the rest of you."

Tom mumbles an apology. The sailor has crossed the line, and he knows it, but that doesn't stop his angry scowling, his eyes from burning a hole right through me. Then I remember the bag of coins. "I'm not a stowaway, Sir, I can pay my way."

Captain Smith counts the money and tucks the sack deftly into his pocket. "There's not enough here to buy you passage to Dublin, let alone Quebec, so you'll have to work to make up the difference. You'll bunk in the mess with the cook and help him with his duties. Welcome aboard the *Sylph*. Now go with Tom. He'll be happy to find you a blanket and some other things you'll need for the voyage. Won't you, Tom?"

Without another word, the captain walks away, leaving me

in Tom's charge. "Come along, stowaway," says Tom sullenly. "Your tale may have softened the old man's heart, but don't expect any sympathy from me."

He takes me below decks and drops a bundle of gear unceremoniously at my feet. "The bowl, spoon and cup are for your meals, the hammock attaches to the hooks in the hull for sleeping, and this oilskin jacket and hat will keep you dry when you work on deck."

"Thank ye," I say gratefully.

"Don't thank me. They're not mine," snaps the sailor. "They belonged to a mate of mine. He's dead, fell from the rigging and died a month ago. But dead or not, I ain't sure he'd be happy to know the captain gave his things to the likes of you."

Tom reaches into his vest, removes a large knife and waves it menacingly in my face before handing it over. "It's not a toy. A good knife's the most useful tool you can have aboard ship, and you never know when you may need it for protection. After all, there are other things than storms that can kill a man out here."

Chapter 7

AT FIRST THE ROCKING and swaying of the *Sylph* is a pleasant sensation, but by the end of my first evening on board my stomach boils. I grow light-headed and am soon sicker than I've ever been before. I spend hours leaning over the railing, emptying my guts into the sea. The worst of all are the laughs and comments from Tom and the rest of the crew.

"How art thee, lad?" asks Francis, the ship's cook, the next day.

"Horrible. Just the thought of food makes me sick. How am I supposed to help make breakfast fer thirty men?" The ship's menu of salt beef and hard biscuits are not to my taste. Indeed, nothing about life at sea seems to agree with me.

"Don't worry, lad," Francis replies in a thick Cornish accent, his mouth barely visible behind his white beard. "You'll be right by 'n by. Every one of us has been sick at sea, even the lads who are teasing you. Thy body just needs time, so make sure you drink a lot of water and keep your innards as full as you can."

"How can I even think about food right now?" I moan.

"Because if you don't, you'll start feeling all shrimmy, and then you're likely to catch something far more serious than seasickness. When people are stuffed together on a ship, disease finds its way on board, and when we arrive in Dublin tomorrow you'll see what I mean. We're gonna be packed tight."

We reach the Port of Dublin just after sunrise. We tie up at the dock, and a few hours later I watch curiously from the deck as the *Sylph*'s Irish passengers come aboard. They are a mix of single young men, families and old couples. Once on board they huddle nervously on the deck, awaiting instructions.

The Irish look utterly destitute, no doubt having spent every penny they had to make the trip, and it appears that the only thing of value they have is the hope that burns brightly in their eyes at the thought of going to Quebec.

I still don't know exactly where Quebec is. I've asked about it several times since leaving Liverpool, but all I've learned is that it's a city in a place called Canada, far away on the other side of the Atlantic.

"My name is Captain Isaiah Smith," the captain says when all the passengers are aboard. "On this ship my word is law.

You are no longer people but cargo, and 'tis my job to get cargo to its destination as quickly and as safely as possible. As such, my rules are few but absolute."

Captain Smith pauses to let the weight of his words sink in. "There are to be no fires on this ship. Ever. You'll not interfere with my crew, and you'll obey the orders of each and every one of them as if they came from me. Finally, in the event of bad weather, you'll be locked in the hold and there you'll stay until either the storm passes or we sink to the bottom of the sea."

A collective gasp rises from the deck as Captain Smith presses on, a grim smile on his face. "Some call these vessels coffin ships," he says coldly, "but the *Sylph* will not be your casket. Should you die on your way to Quebec, so be it. If you do, we'll offer up a prayer for your soul, throw your body overboard and continue on our way. Now make yourselves ready. We sail at once!"

Pushed by a strong wind, the *Sylph* leaves the docks. As the ship bobs westward on the waves, I slowly begin to feel comfortable in my role of assistant ship's cook, thanks in part to Francis's patient tutoring.

"I never set out to be a cook, and the men would tell you I ain't so good at it," Francis says as we clean up the breakfast dishes several days out to sea. "I used to be a grand deckhand though, spending my days one hundred feet above the deck until this happened." Francis holds up his left hand and shows me three short stumps where fingers used to be. I'd noticed the injury earlier but had not thought it proper to ask.

"Caught my hand between a spar and a rope; flesh and bone loses every time that happens. With my hand like this, I weren't much use in the rigging anymore, but I'd sailed with the cap'n since I left Cornwall twenty years ago, and he found a place for me in the galley."

Work done, we walk up the steep stairs to the deck. Francis sniffs the air. "Look to the sky, lad; the clouds are banked up. It will blow a gale before evening so you'd best get some rest. It's gonna be a long night."

By late afternoon the crisp wind that has pushed us far into the Atlantic is gone. The sea is flat and eerily still and the sails dangle slack from their spars. Black clouds hang overhead, swollen with rain, and thunder rumbles across the ocean, each peal perceptibly louder than the one before.

Captain Smith soon confirms Francis's fears. "We're in for some nasty weather," he announces to the hastily assembled migrants. "There's not a ship more seaworthy than the *Sylph*, but for your own safety and that of my crew you'll be locked in the hold until the storm passes. You will not for any reason come back on deck until I give my permission."

There is no argument from the scared passengers, and when the last migrant disappears in the hold, Tom slides a wooden beam noisily across the hatch and bars it shut. "Didn't used to lock 'em in until a few years back when a migrant went crazy down there. He came back up on deck for some reason, tried to grab the ship's wheel. We were rolling and pitching through waves thirty feet high. Had the lunatic managed to turn us we'd have been broadsided and foundered for sure. There was nothin' else for me to do but throw him over the side."

An evil grin crosses Tom's face before he leaves to complete his chores. "So if I were you I'd stay out of my way unless you want to go overboard, too."

Captain Smith raises his voice above the gathering storm. "Furl the sails, secure everything and extinguish the cooking fire. You know your duties, lads, and if you want to stay alive I expect you to fulfill them."

"Don't worry," says Francis. "The *Sylph*'s an ugly old coal barque but she's survived worse than this."

"What do we do?" I ask nervously.

"You'n me will batten the hatches while the men bring down the canvas. Having sails up in a gale is lunacy; the wind would shred 'em to pieces, or they'd hold and the force of the wind would snap the masts or pitchpole us, flip us stern over bow. There ain't nothing we can do but run the wind."

My fear grows like the waves that smack harder and harder against the side of the ship. "Run the wind? What does that mean?" I ask.

"We abandon our course, keep the wind at our back and go wherever the storm takes us. With a smidgeon of luck the cap'n will keep us in a straight line and we should survive. Hurry now, Duncan," Francis says as a peal of thunder explodes overhead. "Things are about to get nasty."

Chapter 8

WHEN THE STORM hits, Francis and I are sent below decks, but we haven't been below more than two hours when the hatchway is thrown open and a sailor, soaked with spray and rain, yells down. "We're taking on water! Get to the pumps!"

"Quickly, lad, don an oiler," says Francis putting on a waterproof coat. "She'll be wild out there."

We quickly climb the wooden steps to the violently pitching deck. Huge waves crash over the rails, and I stagger, nearly losing my footing. Francis's strong hand shoots out and steadies me before I fall. "On the double! The pumps are this way!"

Waves as high as the deck boil black and deadly, threatening to shatter the *Sylph* into pieces. "Hurry! She's filling!"

shouts a sailor. "Pump or we're done for!"

I take my spot at the pumps. The large hand crank is by the main mast and is connected to chains and buckets that run through wooden tubes down to the bilge where they pick up excess water and dump it overboard.

"Enjoying yourself, stowaway?" asks Tom, one of several sailors already pumping furiously. But there's no time for insults. With water pouring into the ship, we're in serious danger of sinking.

The sky, dark all day, grows darker still with the approach of night. I'm drenched from the rain and the cold spray of the Atlantic. My arms and back are numb with pain, but I keep pumping for what seems like hours. "Well done, lad!" says Francis. "Hang on just a little while longer — we're sure to be relieved soon."

"Aye, not bad for a stowaway," says Tom with what appears to be grudging respect. "I might not toss you over the rails after all." Before I have time to reply, a sudden vicious gust of wind hits the ship. It lurches forward and a sickening cracking sound comes from the main mast high overhead.

Above the wind a sailor screams: "Run! The top spar's snapped!" The sailors leap aside as sails, heavy wooden beams and lines fall from the mast, but I'm frozen with fear and can't move. Francis lunges and shoves me roughly aside just as a large mass of ropes and wooden beams hurtles down to the deck, landing with a crash on the very spot I'd been standing. Dazed, I get to my feet, looking frantically for the old man who has just saved my life.

"Over here!" Tom shouts, standing over a misshapen jumble. "Hurry!" I rush over and help Tom tear frantically at the pile of sails, shattered wood and rope, desperate to get to Francis.

"Nae!" I cry when I pull the last piece of canvas away to see the cook's lifeless body, twisted and broken on the deck, his beard stained with blood. The gale gives me no time to grieve. The ship heaves and rolls violently to port as a large wave engulfs the deck, driving me into the main mast with terrific force. I feel something in my chest crack as the air is pushed out of my lungs.

In agony and hardly able to breathe, I crawl back to my feet to find Francis's body gone, the block and the lines swept from the deck, the man who'd saved my life taken with them as well.

But Francis isn't the only sailor who's vanished. "Help!" I hear the faint cry. Clutching my aching side, I stumble towards the sound. "For God's sake, help me!" It's then I see Tom. He's been swept off the deck and landed in the shroud, the network of ropes off the side of the ship that hold the main mast in place. He lies caught in the webbing, dangling helplessly above the cold sea.

Fighting off the pain in my chest, I stagger to the side of the ship and stretch my hand out over the side. "Hold on!" I cry, but before I can reach him, the ship plunges downward into the trough of another large wave. Tom loses his grip on the shroud and falls. With a frantic lunge, he grabs hold of a stray piece of netting and dangles off the side of the ship, nothing between him and the waves but the spray-filled air.

I wrap my hand around a line tied to a stanchion and step over the railing. Struggling for balance, I lean far over the side, trying not to look at the roiling sea.

Before I can reach Tom, the ship swings again, I lose my grip and fall hard onto the deck. My ribs take the blow and explode in pain once more. I can hardly breathe, nearly passing out from the agony, but somehow find a way to stagger to my feet, stumble back to the ship's side, grasp tightly on the line and extend my hand towards Tom, leaning farther and farther out until I can finally grab hold of his wrist.

The rough hemp rope cuts deeply into my left hand and with the large sailor hanging on my right I feel as if my arms are being pulled out of their sockets. I squeeze hard on Tom's wrist, desperate to keep the sailor from falling, but his skin is slippery and slowly, relentlessly, he starts to slip through my fingers. "Don't let go, for God's sake!" he pleads but there's nothing I can do, and I know he's only seconds from sliding out of my hand and into the black water below.

Suddenly strong arms wrap around my waist. "Hang on, boy, I've got you!" A sailor holds me fast while another grabs Tom by his belt, drags him over the railing and pulls him to safety.

Slumping on the deck beside me, Tom wheezes, "Seems the cap'n was right to keep you aboard, stowaway. You found a way to earn your passage after all." It is the last thing I hear before my eyes close and the world goes dark.

Chapter 9

I TRY TO SIT UP from the bed where I'm lying but quickly abandon the attempt, my chest aching too badly to move. And then I see that Tom's injured as well. The sailor's right arm is splinted and bound tightly to his body, a frightful-looking bruise blossoming on his face.

"Storm broke my arm. The ship's surgeon knows his craft well and we'll both heal nicely, but we're going to be awfully sore for the next couple of weeks." Tom grimaces as he shifts his arm. "The gale blew itself out just a few hours ago. You missed the worst of it, been out cold all night, you have. With my arm in this state I wasn't much use on the deck, so the cap'n put me in here to keep an eye on you. He's well impressed with you as well. Not many seasoned sailors, let alone a stowaway, would hang off the side of a ship in a storm like that for another man, especially in the state you were in. I have been told you have some cracked ribs, so you'll have to move slowly for a while."

"Ye say I was out all night?" I ask, confused.

"Aye," says Tom. "Took that long for you to come round. I'm glad you did, though. I owe you an apology. I wasn't very kind when you came aboard. You had no reason to risk your neck for me. Thank you."

Tom helps me to my feet and we step out into the grey morning light to see that the *Sylph* has suffered significant damage in the storm. The top spar has shattered and a network of ropes and sails dangle limp and tattered from the main mast. High above the deck, sailors are hard at work repairing the damage while others stand anxiously near the steerage hatch. I stand for a moment looking out over the sea, which is now rolling in quiet swells. I think again of my sister and wonder if she is all right, if she had, by any chance, been thinking of me during the storm.

"It's time to check on the Irish," Tom says. "Lord knows what happened down there, but as bad as it's been above decks, it will have been far worse below. With the storm, every man was needed to keep the ship afloat; we've had no time to see how the migrants fared."

With a nod from the captain, a sailor opens the hatch. "It reeks!" he cries. "May God have mercy on them!"

In the misery of the hold, the storm has taken a terrible

toll. For two days the migrants have gone without food or water, the buckets used as toilets have spilled and just as Francis prophesied, illness has found its way on board. Four people, three of them babies, died during the storm, the other, a young woman.

The funeral for the migrants, and for Francis as well, is a simple affair. For Francis, whose body was swept overboard in the storm, there is a prayer. For the migrants, Captain Smith reads the few words of committal, then the crew and passengers sing a hymn as the canvas-wrapped bodies, weighted down with ballast stones, are tossed overboard.

A painful memory of my parents sweeps over me. Despite myself I start to cry. "Save your tears," says Tom as the bundles hit the water with hardly a splash. "More will die before this crossing is over."

Tom is right. At least a dozen men, women and children lie wracked with fever down below. The surgeon can do little with such a fever; there's nothing anyone can do. Within the week, eight more shroud-covered bodies slide silently into the deep.

Two weeks after the last funeral, an island appears. At least I think it's an island until the ship creeps closer to the large mass, and I realize it isn't land at all but ice, a floating mountain of ice that towers above the ship. Soon there are more, some no bigger than a rowboat but many others that dwarf the *Sylph*.

"Icebergs. They break free from the northern sea and float

south with the current this time of year," says Tom. "We try to stay as far away from them as possible. They've sunk many ships in these waters, but the storm blew us off our regular course so the cap'n's got no choice but to pick our way slowly through them."

On a quiet evening several days after the encounter with the icebergs, the lookout shouts triumphantly from high above the deck of the ship. Land, he cries, pointing at a distant purple mass on the horizon. We've been expecting the sighting. Shore-clinging seabirds flew overhead earlier in the day, and a small fishing sloop sailed past us just a few hours ago.

"Thank goodness we're here," says Tom. "There were times during that storm I doubted we'd ever see land again."

"Is the ship returning to England soon?" I ask.

Tom laughs. "We've not even docked in Quebec, and you want to cross the Atlantic again? After all you've been through? Why?"

"My sister. She needs my help." It's been six weeks since I've seen Libby, and I am consumed with worry for her.

"Not for a while, I'm afraid. We'll be picking up a load of timber in Quebec and taking it to Jamaica where the cap'n will find a load of sugar or rum bound for England. It could be six months or more until we see Liverpool again."

"Do ye think the captain would take me on until we sail back home?" A delayed passage to England is better than none at all, I tell myself.

Tom shakes his head. "You can't go back to Liverpool yet, Duncan. You're still a wanted man, and I can guarantee that one of the men on board would betray you as soon as we docked in Liverpool. Five guineas is a fortune for a sailor; not many men could say no to it. You need to stay here, let people forget about you."

"So I'm stuck?" I say, trying to keep my emotions in check.

"Don't worry, Duncan. I'm sure by next year it'll be safer for you to return home and look for your sister."

"Home?" I say bitterly. "I don't have a home — all I have is Libby, and she needs my help now. If I don't get back to Liverpool soon, I'm afraid I'm never going to see her again."

Chapter 10

THE SHORE CLOSES in as we sail past a large island full of tall trees, high cliffs and beautiful sand-filled beaches. It still feels like the sea to me, but we're now sailing into the mouth of the St. Lawrence River, Tom says.

Fishing boats and British warships — their sides bristling with cannons — patrol the river, while small farms, neat and orderly strips of land thick with the green growth of late spring, line the bank.

As the sun sets, the *Sylph* enters a large bay, and Captain Smith orders the anchor dropped for the night. River or not, the St. Lawrence is still a dangerous waterway, and he isn't about to risk grounding his vessel this close to our destination.

"Can ye tell me more about Quebec?" I ask the next morning as the ship carries on its way. "I had never heard of the place until I came on board."

"Quebec is a city in Lower Canada, one of our colonies, Duncan, and though we lost the last war with the Americans we managed to beat the French — not that you'd know it. Almost fifty years later, Quebec is still more French than English, although you Scots are doing your best to change that."

The *Sylph* approaches a small island and ties up at a dock. On the shoreline sits a collection of brick and wooden buildings, a cluster of naval cannons and a church.

"This is Grosse Île," says Tom. "Doctors come on board to inspect the passengers and crew. The authorities won't let anyone with typhus, cholera or consumption enter the city. They're quarantined here until they recover or..." Tom doesn't need to finish his sentence and instead points to a large church graveyard, several fresh piles of dirt clearly visible.

At the captain's orders, Irish migrants and sailors alike line up for inspection. Several doctors board the ship, accompanied by a few masked soldiers, and I stiffen as they approach. The doctors inspect the passengers and crew, and although most are allowed to remain on the ship, twelve Irish migrants are tearfully gathered up, placed under guard, and marched down the gangway. As my turn approaches, I pray the soldiers don't know who I am and that the doctors won't find some reason for me to join the sick.

"Your breath sounds laboured, boy — don't have consumption, do you?" a doctor queries.

I lift up my shirt. "Nae, Sir. There was a storm at sea and I got hurt." The doctor studies my bruised chest and sides and after a few seconds steps away, satisfied.

A dozen passengers lighter, the *Sylph* continues its journey, and as the sun starts to dip, we reach Quebec. The city seems small compared to Glasgow. It is a compact place of brick and wood buildings, houses and church spires packed tightly together on narrow streets, nestled between the river and a large hill. "Would you like one last piece of advice before you go?" asks Tom as the ship docks.

"Please," I say gratefully.

"Don't stay in Quebec City," he tells me. "Go upriver to Montreal instead. Montreal's a bigger place and it's full of Scots. I've a mate with a river boat and he'd be glad to take you, I'm sure. And who knows, he may even be looking to hire someone who knows his way around a ship. Come with me and I'll introduce you."

Tom walks me towards another boat tied up a hundred yards or so downriver. It's called the *Montcalm*, a sturdy river freighter that plies the waters between Quebec City and the city of Montreal, explains Tom. As we walk down the dock, John Davis, its master, a tall dark-haired Scotsman greets us warmly.

"Going upriver are ye, lad?" he asks, after Tom makes introductions and tells him I'm looking for passage. "Well, any friend of Tom's is a friend of mine. I'll gladly take ye. We sail as soon as my crew load up the cargo, so why don't ye head to the boat and give them a hand."

"I don't think he's up to much heavy lifting, John," says Tom. "He saved my life on board and took a nasty thrashing to his ribs for his troubles."

"Och! So this brave young man is a hero, is he?" grins Davis.

I blush. "Nae, Sir. We were caught in a storm and I did what anyone else would do in that situation."

"Don't listen to him," says Tom. "The lad risked his life for mine and I owe him a debt. This crossing was the worst I've experienced yet."

"'Tis been bad on the sea of late," Davis agrees. "The *Sylph*'s a guid ship and she can ride out most gales, but there were others not as lucky as ye. Another Liverpool ship, this one bound fer Boston, went down with all hands in the same storm that caught you."

"What was it called?" I ask as a sick feeling grows in my stomach.

"The *Leopard*, I think," says Davis. "Why?"

The *Leopard*. Five minutes quicker and I'd have been on board. I think immediately of the young boy who'd dreamed of a new life with his family, now lost at sea.

"Are ye all right, lad?" asks Davis. "Ye look as if ye've seen a ghost." When I tell the story, Davis lets out a long soft whistle. "Well now, it seems ye have a guardian angel. Say a few prayers fer those poor souls if ye must, but count yer lucky stars and move on. Life is hard. Ye can't enjoy the present if ye wallow in the past."

The *Montcalm*'s cargo consists of supplies destined for the North West Company, and I'm very curious to know what sort of business needs such an eclectic assortment of blankets, tools, buttons and a crate that contains some rather odd-looking metallic jaws.

"They're traps fer catching beaver and other such furry animals," says Davis. "The North West Company's in the fur-trading business. They've a network of posts that reach more than a thousand miles into the western wilds."

"Have ye been out west, Mr. Davis?" I ask.

"Gracious nae! Montreal's as remote a place as I want to go. Only the voyageurs travel that far into the bush. Each one o' them's crazier than the next!"

"Voyageurs? Who are the voyageurs?" The strange word rolls uncomfortably off my tongue.

"I don't have the words to describe them, lad," laughs Davis. "When we get to Montreal ye can see fer yerself." Davis shows me a small rise above the city. "'Tis the Plains of Abraham, where General Wolfe defeated General Montcalm in the battle fer Quebec."

"Why would ye name this boat after a French general?" I ask. "Aren't they our enemy?"

"Not any longer here in the new world. Now we work alongside them. Besides, many of my customers are French so it makes guid business sense. And don't forget I am a Scot;

I bear no love fer the English." The sentiment is one I can sympathize with. Hamilton, Tinker and the soldier who took my sister were English.

"Right, lad," says Davis motioning to the boat. "Say yer goodbyes. 'Tis time to head upriver. It's not as dangerous a trip as across the Atlantic, but it's still no easy matter to get to Montreal."

Tom shakes my hand warmly. "Good luck, Duncan. Things will work out, I know it. Thanks again for saving my life. I'll never be able to repay you, but consider this a start." Before we sail Tom hands me a familiar leather pouch.

"The cap'n said to give you back your money, plus half a pound extra: payment for your services on the ship. Do you still have the knife I gave you?" he asks.

"Aye," I reply, showing him the weapon.

"Good," Tom says from the dock. "You'll need it. Canada is a bit of a wild place."

Chapter 11

THE TRIP UPRIVER to Montreal is uneventful. I try to take a turn on the oars, but my ribs quickly beg me to stop, so for the most part I nestle in a comfortable pile of sacks, alone with my thoughts.

It is now seven weeks since I left Liverpool. I have no idea what's happened to Libby. Every time I think about her, I am worried sick. Tom's warning aside, I need to earn enough money to go home as soon as I can. The thought of waiting a year is simply unbearable.

Three days later the *Montcalm* slips into a Montreal dock. "Do ye have any prospects?" asks Davis. "I'd offer ye a job myself, but I don't have any openings at the moment."

"Nae, I don't." I try to keep the disappointment out of my voice. "Tom thought I might get on with ye."

"I still may be able to help," says Davis. "We're at the North West Company's pier; their office is just up the riverbank. The Company may be looking fer new employees. Come with me and I'll put in a guid word fer ye."

We walk up the dock where I see some of the wildest looking men I could imagine. They have long hair and beards, and are dressed in a combination of animal skins and brightly coloured sashes wrapped around their waists. "Voyageurs?"

Davis laughs. "Aye. I said ye'd have to see them with yer own eyes, didn't I? Normally they're upcountry this time of year, but there's always a few hanging about headquarters. I'm going to introduce ye to Henry Mackenzie. He's the chief clerk of the Montreal headquarters, and he'll decide if ye have a future with the Nor'Westers or not."

We enter a large office and walk up to a bespectacled man with a bushy moustache who sits writing in a book behind a large desk. "Guid evening, Mr. Mackenzie," Davis says, passing the man a piece of paper. "Your shipment from Quebec is here."

Henry Mackenzie looks up from his ledger. "Ah, Mr. Davis. On time as usual, I see."

"Do ye want to inspect the cargo before ye sign the bill of lading, Sir?"

"Not necessary, Mr. Davis," he says, signing the paper with a quill. "In all the years I've known you, you've never been short a nail." Mackenzie unlocks a drawer in the desk and withdraws a handful of silver coins. "Payment in full. Who's the lad?" Mackenzie asks, looking sharply at me.

"Duncan Scott. Just in from the Old Country and looking fer a job. I was hoping ye'd have something." When Davis mentions my name I flinch, wishing I'd had the opportunity to come up with an alias. Goodness knows who is looking for me, even across the Atlantic.

"We can always use a good strong back in the warehouse," says Mackenzie. "Not sick are you? Didn't catch cholera on the crossing?"

I shake my head vigorously. "Nae, Sir, I'm in guid shape except fer my ribs. They took a hit during a storm."

"The lad's being modest, Henry," says Davis. "He earned those cracked ribs saving a sailor's life."

Mackenzie nods approvingly. "So where's your family, lad? You seem a wee bit young to come over by yourself."

"I'm sixteen," I say, more defensively than I'd planned. "I'm here by myself; my parents are dead."

"I'm sorry for your loss, son," he says sympathetically. "You look as if you need a break, so if Mr. McGillivray approves, you're in. Normally he leaves the hiring to me, but he does like to meet potential employees when he has the opportunity."

Henry Mackenzie snaps his fingers, and a boy of about my age runs into the office. "Bring Mr. McGillivray," says Mackenzie. The boy turns and scampers away as quickly as he'd entered at the command. "Well, my lad, we'll soon find out if you've got a future with the North West Company, won't we?"

"I wasn't expecting this," whispers Davis. "Laird William's in charge of the whole Company. He's the most powerful man in Montreal. His influence extends west to the Pacific Ocean and east to London so ye'd best impress him."

A tall and powerful-looking man with long sideburns and red hair strides purposely into the office. "What is it, Mackenzie?"

"This young man's named Duncan Scott. He's been recommended to us by Davis, the shipper, Sir."

"Mr. Davis, how are you?" asks McGillivray warmly, shaking the riverman's hand. "Do you vouch for this boy?"

"Aye, Sir. I'd hire him myself if I had a position."

"You're Scottish so that bodes well," says McGillivray turning to look closely at me, "and you seem strong, but Montreal's full of strong men. Tell me, what can you offer the Company they can't?"

I answer quickly. "Sir, I can read and write so I'd be able to keep records, copy letters, whatever ye need me to do."

"Splendid!" booms McGillivray. "We need men in this operation who can do more than load a bale of furs in a canoe. Welcome to the North West Company!"

"Thank ye, Sir," I say solemnly, shaking McGillivray's offered hand. "I promise I won't let ye down."

"I certainly hope not, lad. Now come with me — you have a lot to learn."

Chapter 12

THE NORTH WEST COMPANY exists because of hats, I learn soon enough — hats made from the exquisite soft inner fur of the beaver pelt, hats wealthy gentlemen across Europe are prepared to pay great sums of money to possess. Vast fortunes are to be made supplying this demand and the Nor'Westers, the men of the North West Company, work hard to ensure they belong to them and not their arch-enemy, the Hudson's Bay Company.

By law, the Hudson's Bay Company owns the vast inland sea they've taken their name from, and in an attempt to squeeze out the competition, the Bay men strictly prohibit the Nor'Westers from sailing into it. The move has outraged the North West Company who must travel twice as far overland as the Bay men because of it. The two companies are engaged in a vicious struggle for control of the fur trade, and violence between them, I discover, is not uncommon.

I learn this and many other things through the spring and summer. I'm taught how to organize a warehouse, value beaver, muskrat and mink skins. I study the Company's map, committing to memory the names and locations of our far-flung trading posts.

The months pass slowly and as the maple and oak trees turn brilliant shades of orange and red, a wave of dismay sweeps over me. By mid-November I've managed to save barely half the money required for passage back to England, and when the last ship to England sails without me, I feel more helpless and alone than ever before. I'm stuck for at least another six months in Montreal, with no way to find my sister.

Winter arrives and brings with it cold and snow unlike anything I ever experienced in Scotland. Nevertheless, the huge snowdrifts that build up along the streets of Montreal are little more than curiosities. I waste precious little time on the weather. I work diligently, but shut in because of the cold, with little distraction, I find that one thought begins to trouble me: Libby, surrounded by soldiers on the dock while I hid in the boat.

"Coward" the soldier had called me. My shame grows by the day as the weight of that word bears down on me. Libby saved my life and in her greatest moment of need I abandoned her.

The winter crawls slowly along, and as the days pass, both my savings and optimism grow. Another two months, maybe three, and I'll be able to go home. When I'm not working, finding my sister is all I can think about — until one rainy March morning when I'm called into Henry Mackenzie's office.

To my great surprise the director of the North West Company is in the office, waiting to speak to me. "Thank you for coming so promptly, Duncan," says McGillivray. "We've been most impressed with your work, and I have a proposition for you. How does a trip to Fort William for the Rendezvous sound?"

Almost two months away on the north shore of Lake Superior, Fort William is the Company's inland headquarters. Early each summer, the Nor'Westers gather at the fort to make deals, establish policies and procedures and to socialize. I know it's a privilege to be asked, but going to the Rendezvous is a dismal prospect. Going west means postponing my trip back to England by four months, maybe even five.

"Laird William, I'm honoured, but isn't there someone more experienced?" I stammer.

McGillivray raises his eyebrow. "I hope you're not refusing an assignment, lad. There's a confidential letter I need delivered to Callum Mackay, the chief trader at Fort William. Aye, there are others who could do it, but the letter contains certain information about the security of our possessions in the West, and both the Company and the Crown need it delivered by someone trustworthy.

"I've been watching you," McGillivray continues. "You're bright, you always complete your tasks, and unlike some of the other lads, you keep your own counsel and avoid the temptations of the taverns. You're just the person I need for this important mission."

I can't believe what I'm hearing. I'm two short months away from returning to England and finding Libby. This "honour" is the last thing I need. "Thank ye, Sir," I say, "but I'm not sure I'm the right person fer the job."

McGillivray's voice is soft, but there's no mistaking the iron underneath. "If you're not prepared to undertake this task I fear you'll need to look for a position somewhere else, my lad. We value loyalty above all else in the North West Company, and your loyalty requires you to go to Fort William."

McGillivray stands over me. "There's also the issue of that trouble you found yourself in back in Britain," he says. "Many ships travel between Canada and England, and they carry gossip as well as supplies. More than a few stories about a young Highlander fleeing the King's justice on the Liverpool docks have reached these shores, stories about a young lad who looks just like you."

"I'm not sure I know what yer talking about, Sir," I say weakly.

McGillivray reaches into a desk drawer and pulls out a familiar poster. "It came a few months after you arrived in Montreal. As far as I know it's the only copy in Quebec. My agent on the waterfront was quick to bring it to me."

My knees buckle and I nearly fall over when I stare at the poster. "The artist did a good job I have to say," McGillivray adds. "The picture's quite recognizable."

"Sir, I . . ." Sweat pools on my face and I bow my head, unable to meet his gaze.

McGillivray carefully folds the poster and puts it back in the drawer. "As far as British justice is concerned, you're not in Montreal, and your secret's safe with me. That is of course if you're willing to go to the Rendezvous. I have a confidential letter from the Colonial Office in London that must get to Fort William, and I need you to deliver it. Can I count on you, Duncan Scott? Can the Company count on you? We're both from the Highlands after all, and Highlanders stick together. Don't they?"

Trapped. I don't have enough money to buy passage home, and if I'm fired from the North West Company, I'd be blacklisted, unlikely to find another job. And if Mr. McGillivray should talk to the commander of the British army garrison at Montreal? I feel an imaginary noose tighten around my neck. I don't even want to think about what would happen to me then.

I lift my head and address my employer. "Of course, Laird William. Whatever ye need me to do."

"Splendid!" he says. "You leave for Fort William in a week. Deliver the dispatch safely and I can assure you that anything you may have done in England stays there."

Chapter 13

WE PREPARE TO DEPART from the North West Company warehouse at the village of Lachine, on the western edge of Montreal. A furious set of rapids between Montreal and Lachine makes river travel from the main headquarters far too risky. For generations, the village has been used as staging ground for voyageurs and explorers heading west.

On the riverfront, bales of cloth as well as tools and other metal products are stacked to the gunwales of ten large canoes. Nearly forty feet long, the Montreal canoe, or *canot du maître* as it is called by the voyageurs, carries a crew of sixteen men and is absolutely vital to the Company.

The man in charge of transporting the priceless cargo to

Fort William is Luc Lapointe, a wiry, leather-faced voyageur with a legendary reputation in the Company. In the final moments before departure, the heavily bearded Frenchman is paying close attention to every detail.

"Remarkable craft, *mon ami*," Lapointe says to me in a thick French accent, gently stroking the side of a canoe, his trained eye looking for tears in the birchbark. "*Très fragile* — nothing more than birch skin wrapped around cedar thwarts. A sharp rock would split her in half and a heavy boot would hole her, but this canoe can carry more than six thousand pounds and take a dozen men across the continent then back again if she's treated with respect, *n'est-ce pas?*"

"Ye talk as if it were a person," I say, only half-listening.

"*Mon ami*! Show me a man who can carry one hundred bales on his back for eighteen hours a day! Look after the canoes and they'll see us through to Fort William."

Lapointe reaches into a leather bag and pulls out a small amount of a thick, sticky substance. It's dark brown and bitter-smelling. I can't possibly imagine why the voyageur has such a thing.

"Spruce gum. The bark's sewn together by *watape*, spruce tree roots, and where the bark pieces meet, the seams leak. Without the resin plugging the holes, the canoes would take on water and sink ten minutes after pushing off. No gum? No canoes. No canoes? No fur trade. It's that simple."

Lapointe rubs a handful of the sticky material into a small gap between two pieces of bark. "*Regardez-moi*, Duncan. If you want to survive in the wild, you have a great deal to learn."

But I have no desire to spend more time in the wild than absolutely necessary. I'm no voyageur — just a reluctant messenger — and the way I'm feeling now it hardly matters if my canoe floats or sinks to the bottom of the river. My mood doesn't improve when William McGillivray himself comes down to the dock.

"Give this to Callum Mackay when you reach Fort William," McGillivray instructs me quietly, giving me a small waterproof oilskin bag. As he does, I notice that the director's hand trembles slightly. "The sealed letter inside contains information vital to Crown and Company so whatever happens, do not lose it. Lapointe alone knows you carry an important message, but even he doesn't know what it says. No one is to read it but Mackay. Do you understand? Nobody, including you."

"Aye, I'll keep it safe, Sir," I promise. Reluctant messenger or not, I realize the importance of the job I've been given.

"I know you will, lad," says McGillivray as Lapointe orders the men to the canoes. "Have a safe journey."

"How will I know who Mr. Mackay is?" I ask, climbing into the canoe.

McGillivray laughs. "Don't worry about that! Mackay's unmistakable."

The voyageurs propel the *canots du maître* expertly away from the docks. Lapointe begins to sing and soon the others join in, their voices echoing across the black water. "We're not travelling far today," says Lapointe when the song ends, "just to the village of Sainte Anne de Bellevue."

"But that's only a few hours up the river," I say. "I've studied the Company maps for months. Why are we stopping so soon?"

"We have important business to conduct there," Lapointe explains. "Besides, I wouldn't be in too great a rush if I were you. Sainte Anne's the last taste of civilization many fur traders ever get to enjoy."

Chapter 14

AFTER ONLY A FEW hours on the water, I'm exhausted. A winter keeping ledgers and organizing a warehouse is hardly demanding physical labour, and paddling a loaded canoe is something else entirely. My shoulders and arms ache, and my palms are soon covered in weeping blisters from the butt of the paddle, but my body isn't the only thing that hurts.

It's been nearly a year since I last saw Libby, and my whole soul aches to be sailing across the Atlantic, back to Liverpool. Instead, here I am, travelling farther and farther away from my sister. I paddle in silence, alone in my thoughts, and don't notice the approaching village until the canoes glide to shore on the outskirts of Sainte Anne de Bellevue, shaking me out of my dark mood.

"What about the rum, Luc?" asks a voyageur, referring to a duty the men have been anxiously waiting for Lapointe to complete. Rum, nearly a gallon per man, is traditionally distributed at the start of every trip to celebrate the voyage and to boost morale.

"*Ce soir* — tonight, but first we have spiritual matters to attend to." Leaving one of the paddlers behind to guard the canoes, we walk along a little path to the village. The track widens and turns into a street that leads to a small grey-stone church. I'm surprised at the reverence that sweeps through the men of the brigade as we enter the chapel through the heavy wooden doors.

Although Catholic from birth, the voyageurs hardly ever act in a manner a priest would approve of, but now they've turned into different men altogether. At the front door, Lapointe removes his cloth hat respectfully. "We pray to Sainte Anne and ask her to keep us safe. Do you have any money, *mon ami*?"

I'm not sure why I would need money in the wilderness. "Nae. I left all my money with Henry Mackenzie."

Lapointe hands me a small copper coin. "Place it in the alms box when we go in. It's bad luck not to."

I do as I'm told and line up with the others to receive a blessing from the priest, a gaunt old man with thinning white hair. When each man has received his blessing, we leave the church and return to the canoes. "Are you Catholic, Duncan?" Lapointe asks as we walk back along the path.

"Aye," I say, "though my family only went to the kirk fer St. Andrew's Day and Christmas."

"The only time I step foot in a church myself is here in Sainte Anne," confides Lapointe.

"So why do ye go at all?"

Lapointe smiles cryptically. "You've never travelled in the wilderness, *mon ami*. I know what can happen in the wilds, and believe me, there's nothing wrong with asking for a little *intervention divine*. Out here, a man can use all the help he can get."

Chapter 15

WHEN LAPOINTE DISTRIBUTES the rum I have difficulty believing my riotous companions are the same group of pious worshippers I saw in the church just a few hours before. I receive my own share, but the fiery liquid burns my throat and I spit it out immediately, much to the amusement of the men.

"There's plenty of water in the river if you prefer!" says Pierre Fournier, a likeable voyageur with a thick blonde beard and the best sense of humour in the brigade. I manage a weak smile and give my bottle away, much to the delight of the men who toast my generosity long into the night.

We depart the next morning well before dawn. "We have a long way to go, and rum or not we always start before the sun rises," says Lapointe as the canoes slip out into the black water. "We'll be leaving the St. Lawrence for the Ottawa River around the next bend, and the little farmhouse you'll see on the shore is the last sign of civilization you'll encounter for a long time."

The farm and the mouth of the Ottawa River appear, and on Lapointe's command, we make a hard turn to starboard. The Ottawa's current is strong and I strain to push my paddle through the water. "Does the river get faster than this?" I ask, sweat forming on my forehead.

Lapointe laughs. "This is nothing. Ahead we'll paddle on rivers so fast they make the Ottawa feel like a pond. And that's on a good day. On the bad ones we'll spend our time portaging waterfalls and rapids with nearly two hundred pounds of gear on our backs — and with a canoe high above our heads as well. Enjoy your time on the river; you'll be walking soon enough."

Two days' travel upstream, the gurgling of the Ottawa River grows into a low rumble, a sound that increases to a thunderous roar as we round a turn in the river and see the waterfall. Lapointe shouts above the noise as he directs the brigade to shore. "La Grande Chaudière! The Big Boiler it's called in English," he says. "A remarkable sight, *mais non*?"

I can only nod in amazement as I watch the river tumble violently thirty feet down a series of rocky outcrops, shooting foam high up into the air. "You won't find the waterfall as remarkable as Lapointe says it is in a moment or so," says Fournier, reluctantly stepping out of the canoe onto the riverbank. "We'll soon find out what kind of a voyageur you really are when you start walking."

Fournier lifts a bale onto my back and my legs buckle under the weight. "This will make it a bit easier," he says, wrapping one of the brightly coloured sashes favoured by the voyageurs behind the wooden frame backpack and around my forehead.

"It's called a *ceinture fléchée*, a tumpline," he explains. "It spreads the load evenly across the whole body and lets a man carry more than he weighs — if he uses it well. Look to Lapointe and you'll see what I mean."

I watch as Lapointe walks confidently along the path with three bales on his back, more than two hundred and fifty pounds of gear, secured by his own bright crimson sash.

"We measure portages by how many steps we walk," Fournier says, "and Chaudière has six hundred and forty-three of them. Luc wants the portages to be over as soon as possible so he carries half of the goods on his own to speed things up!"

We walk slowly, carefully placing one foot in front of the other. "Watch your step," Fournier warns. "More than a few men have fallen into the river here. If you slip, throw the gear off your body as quickly as you can before you reach the water; it's better to feel Lapointe's wrath for losing the cargo than flounder at the bottom of the river with the fish!"

We make three trips on the portage. I carry three bales to Lapointe's nine, and when we're finally finished I look at the leader of the brigade with a respect that borders on awe.

Lapointe loads the last bale, looking no more tired than if he'd just returned from a leisurely stroll. "*Allez*! No time to dawdle."

The days soon settle into a steady rhythm. We carry trade goods that the North West Company urgently needs for the upcoming trading season, and we're driven by the knowledge that Fort William, and the Company itself, waits impatiently for our arrival.

Despite my constant yearning to return to England and find Libby, I marvel at the beauty of the land around me. I also discover that I'm quite adept at paddling. "*Bon*! You're doing well," says Lapointe. "We'll make a voyageur out of you yet." I flush with the praise, but when I see the massive body of water that waits for us at the mouth of the French River, all my new-found confidence quickly disappears.

"We need a ship to travel on this! Not canoes," I say, staring at an endless expanse of water.

"Duncan, this is Georgian Bay, only an inlet of Lake Huron," says Lapointe. "Just wait until you see Lake Superior; it makes this place look like a duck pond."

Before we continue, Lapointe and the others ship their paddles and toss coins, buttons and tobacco into the rough water of the lake. "What's that about?" I ask.

"Old Lady Wind, *La Vieille*, will sink us in a heartbeat if we anger her, so we give gifts to keep her happy and as far away from the canoes as possible."

"I thought Sainte Anne protected us," I say.

Lapointe drops another handful of tobacco into the slate-grey water. "I don't think Old Lady Wind knows Sainte Anne. Besides, we're now a very long way away from her church. We're in *La Vieille*'s country now, and I have no problems praying to whoever will help me stay alive."

As we push farther along Lake Huron, I learn the names and uses of all the trees and plants that grow along the lakeshore. Lapointe and the others teach me how to use a flintlock rifle and pistol, and despite my initial doubts at Lachine, I even master the art of waterproofing canoes. But there are also many long hours of silent paddling, and at those times my mind drifts to my family.

I miss my parents terribly, and I'm constantly plagued by the guilt of staying home on the day they died, then abandoning my sister. It's torture to think that if things had gone according to my plans I would have been on a ship by now, eastbound on the Atlantic, instead of travelling west on a lake to the middle of nowhere.

But there is nothing I can do except try to put these thoughts aside and paddle. And paddle we do, day after day, week after week, until just before sunset, six weeks after leaving Montreal, we reach Fort William, a large collection of warehouses, residences and workshops nestled behind enormous wooden palisades on the shores of Lake Superior, a massive lake that more than lives up to its name.

Dozens of canoes, small sailboats and other vessels sit tied up to the long wharf, while even more lie overturned on the shore. Over it all, our flag — a large British ensign on a red background with the Company's initials prominently displayed in white — flutters proudly in the evening wind.

"Travellers!" someone yells as we beach our canoes, and from out of nowhere a score of men scurry down to the shore and greet us with laughs and hugs.

"Food and rum!" cries Lapointe, and once the precious cargo of trade goods is safely unloaded, we're led into the largest log building I've ever seen in my life.

One hundred people or more are already eating in the room Lapointe calls the Grand Hall, but there is still plenty of room for us. Before we can sit, however, a man approaches, easily the largest person I've ever seen, nearly seven feet tall with shoulders the size of kegs and a flaming orange beard that bounces up and down.

"Luc!" The giant shouts in the thickest brogue I've heard since leaving Scotland. McGillivray was right, I see. I know who this man is immediately.

Callum Mackay embraces the voyageur in a crushing bear hug. "Damnation, Luc, but it's guid to see ye again! I feared ye'd grow soft wintering in Montreal!"

"Callum, every now and then even I need a break from the

wild." Lapointe puts his arm around my shoulder. "This is Duncan Scott, and he's got a letter for you."

"The post can wait! It's rum and roast moose that count now!"

"*Non*, Callum, it's from McGillivray. Can we find a quieter place than the Hall? I don't know what the paper says but I know *le patron* wanted you to read it as soon as we arrived."

"His lairdship himself," mutters Mackay, leading us into a small office off the Grand Hall. Mackay shuts the door, unfolds the oilskin, breaks the seal on the letter and reads the contents in silence.

"Most interesting," he says, putting the document down some time later. "Most interesting, indeed. I hope ye enjoyed yer time in Montreal, Luc, because ye've got more o' the bush in front o' ye than ever before. The laird's given Simon Fraser permission to leave Fort St. James and travel the Columbia to finish the job Sir Alex started, and ye get to deliver the news to Fraser personally."

"Alexander Mackenzie? I read about him in Montreal," I say. Sir Alexander Mackenzie's travels in the West have made him a legend in the Company.

"Aye, lad. Fifteen years ago the Knight discovered a large river west of the Rockies. He believed it to be the Columbia and travelled it fer a while, searching out a route to the Pacific, but he abandoned the river not long after. 'Twas far too wild and dangerous, or so Mackenzie claimed. He went o'erland to the ocean instead, on a route too treacherous fer trade.

Fraser always believed Mackenzie exaggerated the dangers. He believes the river's navigable and aims to prove it himself."

"Simon Fraser is our most senior officer west of the Rocky Mountains," says Lapointe. "He's always believed Mackenzie was wrong to give up on the Columbia. He thinks the river will work perfectly well for the Company. More than two years ago he asked permission to travel its length, but was refused. Now it looks like he's going to get his chance to find out.

"And a good thing, too," he continues. "The cost of hauling fur and trade goods from the West to Montreal is bleeding us dry. We need access to the Pacific if we're to survive much longer."

That much I knew. Without access to Hudson Bay, every fur and every axe and bolt of cloth the Nor'Westers carry goes overland to and from Montreal, increasing our costs dramatically. Finding a route to the Pacific has been a Company priority for years.

Mackay lowers his voice and attempts a whisper, no easy feat for the giant. "But that's not the least of it, Luc. McGillivray received a letter from the Colonial Office in London. Apparently the Yanks have set out west to snatch the Columbia fer themselves. Two fellows, Lewis and Clark, have been sent by the president himself. Ye can well imagine that neither the Company nor the Empire is happy about that. Fraser's to ensure the West remains in British hands, and that the Company gets a navigable route to the Pacific."

"*Très bien*," says Lapointe. "Simon will be ecstatic. He's been looking to get his name written in the history books for years. Besides, you know how he feels about the Americans. He'd love to stick it to them."

Mackay looks at me with a twinkle in his eye, and I suddenly feel very uncomfortable. "The laird mentions ye as well, lad. Why do ye think ye were sent here?"

"To bring the letter?" I reply, alarmed.

"Any idiot can deliver the post!" scoffs Mackay. "Nae, laddie, Montreal has greater plans fer ye. 'I'm also sending a young clerk named Duncan Scott,'" Mackay reads, copying McGillivray's patrician voice perfectly. "'Promote him to apprentice clerk and send him west to Fort St. James with Lapointe and the trade goods Fraser will need for this venture. He's an intelligent, hard-working young man, and Simon will benefit from the help.' What do ye think, lad?" asks Mackay. "Fancy a wee trip to the Pacific yerself?"

Send him west. My brain tries to register the magnitude of those three little words. *Send him west.* I thought once I'd reached Fort William I could return home and begin to look for Libby. The new title of clerk means nothing to me. All I know is that I won't be going home for a very long time.

Chapter 16

A LIGHT DRIZZLE FALLS as the Nor'Westers pace the dock anxiously, talking in low murmurs, smoking their pipes. The men are used to long journeys, but with the exception of Lapointe none has travelled as far west as Fort St. James. All are tense as Lapointe orders them to the water.

"*Allez*! It will take four months to reach Fraser, and we won't get there by wasting time in idle chatter." As we head out onto the lake, Lapointe taps me on the shoulder with his paddle. "You don't seem to be very excited about this trip."

I feel as if my heart is dragged down by stones. I'm overwhelmed with frustration and anger that I'm unable to find and help Libby. "I was counting on going back to England after Fort William," I admit. "There are things I have to do."

"Tell me, *mon ami*, what are these 'things' that are so important they weigh you down like this?" Lapointe asks.

"My sister's in trouble and I need to help her." Although I've travelled with Lapointe for almost two months, I've said almost nothing about my family until now.

Lapointe doesn't prod. Instead, he nods knowingly and exhales, pipe smoke rising lazily through the rain. "Family is important, perhaps the most important thing you can have, and if it's meant to be then you will see your sister again, but life sometimes makes other plans for us. Now your destiny's taking you west so make the best of it, or mope. The choice is up to you, but either way you're going to Fort St. James."

With Lapointe's words echoing in my head we travel ever west, traversing immense stretches of rocky tree-covered plateaus. Swamps and small lakes are everywhere and the water is home to moose and beaver and mosquitoes. I hate the voracious little pests and am soon covered in itchy red welts, but the voyageurs don't seem to be bothered nearly as much by the insects, and one night I ask Lapointe why.

"You must smell very tasty to *les moustiques*," he laughs. "Our blood's too old for them, I suppose."

I swat frantically at the cloud of buzzing insects that swarm around my head. "Stop joking!" I cry. "They're driving me mad!"

"Mosquitoes dislike the smoke from our pipes as much as you do," Lapointe says, and I blush. I've tried smoking one of the long pipes favoured by the voyageurs, but it was as unpleasant an experience as the rum. I'd coughed so hard I nearly fell out of the canoe.

"Besides, you wash too much," adds Fournier. "There are no women to impress out here so let yourself get dirty — that will help keep the mosquitoes away as well."

The rocky woodlands finally give way to endless seas of flowing grassland, and more than a month after leaving Fort William, a sense of excitement builds amongst the men.

"What's going on?" I ask, watching as the voyageurs paddle with a renewed energy against the current and the warm summer air.

Even Lapointe can hardly contain his enthusiasm. "*Mon ami*, we're only a little way from Red River. We have friends and family here we haven't seen for a long time. There will be a great celebration when we arrive tomorrow night. We'll sleep in soft beds and eat fresh food, so paddle hard, the Métis await!"

The next evening the canoes glide onto shore at a small settlement at the edge of a grassy plain. A large man with a long black beard and fringed leather jacket pushes his way through the crowd, grabs Luc and me together in one arm and crushes us in an embrace.

"*Bienvenue!*" he shouts as my nostrils fill with the strong scent of leather and smoke. "Welcome to Red River!"

Lapointe extricates himself from the man's grasp. "Duncan, this is Louis Desjarlais, a leader of the Métis. You and I will be staying at his guest house while we're here, so have a wash and change your clothes; there will be a feast tonight!"

As we go off together, I ask Lapointe about the Métis.

The Métis, he explains, are descendants of both the French *coureur de bois* and the original inhabitants of the plains. Apparently they have lived at Red River for generations and have been our partners in the fur trade, supplying us with pemmican. Made from dried buffalo meat, pounded into a powder and mixed with berries and hot fat, pemmican lasts for months and is the staple food of the voyageurs. In fact, we've eaten little but pemmican and pea soup since leaving Fort William. The prospect of the feast Lapointe speaks about is very enticing.

As the sun dips low over the prairie, I dress in my cleanest clothes, leave Desjarlais' guest house, a small sod cabin not much bigger than a chicken coop, and follow the sound of laughter and music to a large crackling bonfire.

A crowd of perhaps two hundred people have gathered. Someone thrusts a plate full of roasted buffalo into my hands and I take a bite of the most delicious meat I've had in my life. "Thank ye, Monsieur Desjarlais," I say to my host. "This is a great dinner."

"My friends call me Louis and you are now my friend. I'm glad you like the meal, but buffalo is more than just food, you know. Our entire way of life depends upon it. As the buffalo fare, so do the Métis."

Desjarlais' brows furrow. "I fear, though, that winds of change are about to blow across this land. I've heard a rumour that the Bay men plan on bringing settlers to our valley, people who would take our land and farm it."

Desjarlais spits out the word as if it were a fly that he'd just swallowed. "Farmers! They would descend like grasshoppers, the buffalo would disappear, and we would have to fight for our very lives." The Métis leader grows silent for a moment and looks away into the darkness.

"Forgive me. I speak of rumours and gossip, and I'm not being much of a host. Tonight we won't worry about the future. Instead we will sing, dance and tell stories far into the night!"

Desjarlais is true to his word, and I eat far more than I ever thought possible. After dinner, fiddles and harmonicas emerge, and the crowd erupts in dance. At first I sit by the fire, content just to watch, until a young girl appears out of nowhere and extends her hand invitingly.

"I . . . I don't dance," I stutter awkwardly.

The girl grabs my hand and pulls me off my feet with more strength than I would have thought possible from such a tiny frame. "Everyone dances at Red River! My name's Louise," she says, putting her arms around my waist.

"I'm Duncan," I tell her. "I've never danced before and don't have a clue what I'm doing."

"I know who you are," she says. "You're staying in my guest house! Louis is my father." She lifts up my hand, spins in a tight circle and pulls me along to the beat of the music. "You're doing very well for someone who doesn't dance, by the way!" she says as my face erupts in a smile.

After much dancing, I go to bed late. When I wake up the next morning I have nothing pressing to do, and so I go for a walk around the small community. I've hardly gone more than fifty paces when I encounter my dance partner from the night before.

Louise stands smiling on the path, the reins of a large coal-black horse in her hand. "I enjoyed spending time with you last night," she says. "I hope you got enough rest?"

I blush. "I slept fine, thank ye."

"My father said it would be all right if I stole you away and showed you the country around Red River. You've ridden before, haven't you?"

As a child I rode on the backs of the stocky Highland ponies that pulled plows in the rocky fields of Scotland, but the massive beast grazing contentedly behind Louise is no pony. Muscles ripple under its jet-black skin and it towers over every horse I've ever seen.

"Once or twice," I say cautiously, "but I'm not much guid at it."

Louise jumps gracefully onto the horse's back. "If I can teach you to dance I can certainly show you how to ride. *Allons-y*! Kavalé's strong enough to carry the both of us."

There's no saddle or stirrup to help me onto the horse and it takes a strong arm from Louise to get me seated behind her. She turns to me and grins when I've mounted. "Now whatever happens, hold on!"

With a sharp prod of her heels, Louise urges Kavalé on,

and the horse surges forward. I wrap my arms tightly around Louise's waist to stop from falling as Kavalé thunders across the prairie, turf flying from his hooves.

"Not that hard," she laughs. "I can barely breathe!" Reluctantly I relax my grip and open my eyes. I've never travelled this fast before. The sensation of speed is thrilling. We gallop for a few exhilarating minutes until Louise eases the horse back into a trot. "What do you think of Kavalé?"

"He's marvellous!" I say, catching my breath.

"I think so, too. Kavalé's my best friend. His name means 'sweetheart' in Michif, our language. I named him that when I was seven and he was just a colt."

The air on the prairies is thick with the scent of wildflowers and grasses. With no mountains or buildings to block the horizon, the sky seems endless. Small white clouds float lazily past and the early summer sun beats down on my face. After a while Louise stops the horse and we dismount.

She points to a plant that reminds me of the stunted barley that grew in the stony ground of our farm in Loch Tay. "It's called sweetgrass and it's one of our most sacred things," she says. "It may not look very special on the outside, but it holds great power within. People are like that too. I think you have something special within you, Duncan, and I'd like to hear how you came to be at Red River."

Something gives inside of me. "The last time I saw my sister was on a dock in Liverpool," I say as the words I've kept deep in my heart tumble out like water from a spring. "I hid like a coward. That was what the soldier called me, and he was right; I was a coward! I stayed on the ship and did nothing while they took her away. Now I'm stuck here and I can't get back home to help her."

Louise listens intently. "I don't think you are a coward at all," she says when I finish my story.

"How can ye say that?" I ask. "I abandoned my sister!"

"It was an impossible situation you were in," says Louise. "Your sister knew that. She made a choice to save your life. You could have tried to help her, but it wouldn't have made any difference to her fate, and her sacrifice would have been wasted. Instead, you're alive. You will find her one day, I know it."

Louise strokes my cheek and my skin burns from her touch. "Life is a terribly fragile thing, Duncan," she says. "The ones we love can be taken away in a heartbeat. Ten years ago my mother died in childbirth. I lost her and a little brother I never came to know. I could have let my pain destroy me, but what good would that have done? Fate may decide what happens, but we are the ones who can choose how to respond. I chose to live — and you should too."

Louise takes my hand and we walk up a small rise. When we reach the top of the hill, Louise points excitedly to the horizon. "Buffalo!" she says. "Look!" To the west are thousands of enormous shaggy brown beasts milling about on the prairie. I've never seen so many animals in my life and am amazed at the size of the herd.

"We'll go on a hunt soon. Perhaps you could stay and join us?" Louise's eyes sparkle at the prospect.

I shake my head sadly. "I'd like that very much but we're leaving tomorrow. Lapointe and I have a long way to go."

Louise's disappointment is evident. "That's the way of you fur traders. Always travelling, never in one place long enough to call it home. Speaking of home," she says, "it's time for us to get back. My father must be told about the buffalo."

When we arrive back at Red River, Louis Desjarlais greets the news of the buffalo with great excitement. As predicted, a hunt is planned for the following day. We are asked if we will join, but with reluctance Lapointe declines, well aware of the importance of the letter I carry for Simon Fraser.

"I'm sorry, my friend, but we've no choice. Duncan and I have important business in the West. We must leave before we become too fat and lazy to paddle."

"Then tonight we'll feast!" the Métis leader exclaims. "And we'll send you on your way with full bellies."

Desjarlais is true to his word and although the night is once again filled with food and music, it is not nearly as enjoyable as the first one I spent at Red River. Hours go by. Louise doesn't appear and it isn't until I'm about to go to bed, bitterly disappointed, that she finally arrives by the fire, a small bundle in her hands. "Where were ye?" I ask. "I waited all night to see ye."

"I'm sorry but I was making this for you," she says. "I wanted to finish it before you left." Louise holds up a small leather pouch, beautifully decorated with beadwork and quills. "It's a medicine bag. It's used to carry special things so that you never forget the people or places that are important to you. I've put a pebble from the Red River inside of it already. I want you to always remember this place. And me."

Louise's eyes glisten. "Fill it with the things that mean something to you and tell me all about them when you return."

As if acting by itself, my hand reaches into my jacket and pulls out the embroidery I'd taken from our small apartment in Glasgow. "It's a wee picture of our old home in Scotland," I tell her. "It's nothing like the medicine bag but my mother made it, and it's very special to me. Besides, I think she would have liked ye to have it."

Louise clutches the embroidery tightly in her hand. "I love it — and I like you very much as well, Duncan Scott."

The distance between us closes until our lips softly touch. "Promise you'll return," Louise whispers, breaking the kiss and speeding away.

"Aye," I whisper breathlessly into the cool night sky. "I promise I will."

The sun hasn't climbed above the horizon when I wake. I slept fitfully, and as I walk down to the river I discover that my back and legs ache terribly, the after-effects of riding the horse. I'd not have traded the memory of that day for anything, but I know the canoe ride will be misery.

Desjarlais sees us off. "You're welcome here anytime,

Duncan," he says with a sly grin. "I think my daughter would be very happy if you tired of the fur trade and hunted the buffalo with us!"

Blushing for what seems to be the hundredth time, I load my possessions into the canoe. The medicine bag hangs around my neck on a leather cord, and I feel the weight of it pressing against my heart. I look everywhere for Louise, but she's nowhere to be seen.

Lapointe must read the disappointment on my face. "It's not easy saying goodbye," he says as the canoe enters the dark river. "Many of us have wives and children scattered across this continent, but leaving them comes with the job and you learn to deal with it."

"I just wish I'd seen her one last time, Luc."

Lapointe points his paddle to the bank. "Then stop moping and start looking." Above the river, Louise stands silently in the pre-dawn shadows, holding a lantern above her head. She raises her hand in a wave as we drift past and then she's gone again, swallowed up by the night.

"Put your mind into your stroke and forget about her for now," says Lapointe. "You'll be back in Red River someday, but we've a long way to go through dangerous country, so keep your wits about you. Men who lose focus out here often end up dead."

Chapter 17

AS WE PUSH TOWARDS our goal, a place far to the west called Fort St. James, the grasslands disappear as we enter a landscape carpeted with trees, rivers, lakes and swamps. We continue west through the forest along the great inland highway of the fur trade, the Saskatchewan River, dropping off men, canoes and supplies at Cumberland House, La Loch, Fort Vermilion, Fort Chipewyan and a host of other isolated North West Company outposts.

Two months after leaving Red River, and now paddling on the Peace River, a majestic range of mountains comes into view, their snow-capped peaks so large that the little piles of heath and stone I knew back in Scotland hardly seem worthy of the same name.

"The Rocky Mountains they're called. We will traverse them to the north," says Lapointe. "We've almost made it, *mon ami*. Fort St. James and Simon Fraser are less than three weeks away." ·

We reach Fort Dunvegan, a small post on the banks of the Peace River. Ever mindful of the importance of our mission we stay just two days, then say our goodbyes as Lapointe and I leave in one lone canoe. The other voyageurs remain at Fort Dunvegan, needed for the local fur trade.

We enter the mountains. I feel claustrophobic as we fight against the increasing current of the river, following it into a deep mountain pass. We make many portages around log-jams and rapids, each one more difficult than the last.

Even though our load has been much reduced along the way, our canoe still carries nearly three hundred pounds of supplies: supplies that need to be packed on our backs at each portage.

A week from Fort Dunvegan, and with the western flanks of the mountain behind us, the river widens, slows down and deposits us on the shores of a large lake. Not far from the river mouth is an abandoned collection of log cabins. The door of the largest building hangs limp, partially ripped off its hinges. Judging by the mess inside, a bear or some other large animal has made the place its home, and the destruction mystifies Lapointe.

"This place is called Fort Misery," says Lapointe.

"I can see why," I reply, looking at the wreckage around me.

"The name is more than appropriate in the middle of the winter," agrees Lapointe, "but in the summer it has always been a decent enough place to rest before the final push to Fort St. James. This is valuable fur country; there should be men at this post trading with the local people. I don't for the life of me understand what happened."

Lapointe looks unsettled. "Usually we'd stay and rest here for a day or two, but we'll leave at first light tomorrow. There's no point in lingering in these ruins."

The abandoned fort marks the start of the longest portage on the journey. A trail has been blazed through the woods to guide the few fur traders that venture this far west, but off the narrow path the wilderness is dark and oppressive. We keep our guns close by.

After three long days of portaging, we reach the banks of a large river. Grateful to be out of the forest, we stop for just a short break before Lapointe orders us onto the water. "Fort St. James is just a few hours upstream. We'll reach it by nightfall if we put our backs into it. *Allez*! I'm tired of sleeping in these cursed woods!"

Just before dusk, the canoe enters a large lake surrounded by low rolling mountains. I scan the lakeshore and see a handful of small log cabins with the North West Company's flag fluttering above them. People stand on the beach, and a chorus of shouts fills the air as our canoe crunches loudly on the gravel. Within seconds we're surrounded by a smiling and shouting crowd.

"They are the Carrier people," says Lapointe, exchanging a

few strange guttural words with a smiling man. "Fraser named the place Fort St. James, but these people call it Nak'azdli."

"Let me through!" A powerful voice shouts from beyond the circle of well-wishers, and the man I've crossed a continent to see strides purposefully through the crowd.

Simon Fraser is a short, compact man with large auburn sideburns that reach down to his prominent chin. I'm surprised at his age. Fraser is barely in his thirties by the looks of things, and though I'd not consider the explorer a handsome man, there's something captivating about him. Simon Fraser is a man to be reckoned with, I can tell.

"It's good to see you again, Simon," grins Lapointe. "We missed you at the Rendezvous."

"Luc! It's always a pleasure to see you." I'm taken aback by Fraser's voice. With the Scottish name, I'd expected a strong Highland lilt but he speaks with a strange nasal accent. Then his sharp eyes rest firmly on me.

"You have a youngster with you I don't know. What's your name, boy, and what brings you to New Caledonia?"

I reach into my jacket for the precious oilskin-covered package. "My name's Duncan Scott, Sir. Mr. McGillivray sent me to give ye this letter — and to help ye."

As Fraser takes the letter, a short, wiry man with a close-cropped black beard and eyes that shine like coal steps forward, leering in a way that makes me shudder.

"Help us? You hardly look old enough to dress yourself!" The man edges closer. This isn't the greeting I'd expected, and my cheeks turn red in anger.

"That's enough, La Malice," Fraser says, stuffing the letter in his vest. "You'd do well to watch your tongue."

"My apologies, *Monsieur*," this La Malice says, voice dripping with sarcasm on the word "Monsieur." "I'm certain our new *helper* has a wealth of experience in the bush. I'm more than happy to defer to his wisdom."

Fraser chooses to ignore the comment and instead turns his attention to me. "Well Mr. Scott, since you're here to help, you may as well start by unloading the supplies you have so graciously brought."

Eager to impress, I lift a heavy bale of supplies from the canoe, well aware that the eyes of every voyageur are on me. I struggle with the bale, and as I do, I slip on a wet rock, lose my balance and fall into the cold water of the lake. Cheeks burning with embarrassment I scramble to my feet and heave the wet bale to shore, my ears stinging with La Malice's laughter.

"What did I tell you?" he says. "The little whelp can't even carry a bale from the canoe!"

My temper flares and without thinking I pick up a paddle and splash the mocking voyageur. The crowd erupts in cheers, but La Malice's eyes glitter with hate. "You'll pay for that, boy," the voyageur hisses, his fists clenched.

I easily sidestep the attack. Not expecting me to move so fast, La Malice stumbles and lands heavily in the lake himself. "Who's the drowned rat now?" I shout.

"I'll show you what happens to whelps who don't know their place!" La Malice shouts, climbing quickly to his feet, lunging towards me as his hand moves purposefully towards the large knife in his belt.

Fraser steps between us. "Hold your hand and your tongue, La Malice. You got no more than you deserved. Leave the lad alone and get back to work."

Venom shooting from his eyes, the voyageur splashes out of the water. "You'll regret that, boy," he whispers as he passes by, his breath hot on my cheek.

Simon Fraser slaps me heartily on the back. "You certainly know how to make an introduction, my hot-headed friend. You've won yourself a place with the men, no doubt, but I'd watch out for La Malice if I were you. He's not exactly known for his sense of humour. Now help finish unloading the canoe. Then put on some dry clothes. And this time," Fraser laughs, "try to keep my supplies out of the lake."

As I'm escorted from the beach, Fraser turns to a tall man standing beside him. "After a day or two, Mr. Stuart, once Luc's rested up, ask him to return to Fort Dunvegan with one of the other voyageurs for the winter. Also, bring La Malice to my cabin in half an hour," he adds in a lower tone of voice. "I'll have a stern conversation with him, but first I need a moment's peace to read the letter from Montreal."

Fraser holds the unopened oilskin before his eyes and struggles to control his excitement. "If this says what I hope it does, we'll have far bigger things on our plates than a surly voyageur."

Chapter 18

SIMON FRASER, John Stuart, his second-in-command at Fort St. James, and I face La Malice in the explorer's small log cabin. "Account for your disgraceful behaviour on the beach, La Malice," Fraser demands.

La Malice's eyes narrow. "*Account* for myself, Monsieur? Do you know how long I've been with this Company?"

Fraser's reply is curt. "Your length of service in the North West Company is not the issue. Mr. Scott is an apprentice clerk and as such he outranks you."

"That whelp is to be my superior officer?" La Malice barely contains his anger, his eyes burning into me. "I was trading furs when this boy was still in his crib."

Fraser does his best to control his rising temper. "Clerks are selected by merit, not age, and you'll do well to remember that, La Malice. Your insolence and insubordination ensure you'll never be more than a voyageur. Should you lay one finger on Mr. Scott, I'll see to it personally that your days in the North West Company are over."

Although I appreciate the idea that I outrank La Malice, I am also disturbed that he is obviously so much stronger and more forest-knowledgeable than I am. I want to say something to calm his anger with me but there is no chance.

"There's also the issue of that girl of yours," John Stuart adds. "She hasn't been seen for a while and the locals are talking."

"She's no concern of yours," La Malice replies. "Besides, there aren't any rules in the Company against having a bush wife are there? If there were, I fear you'd be most severely reprimanded yourself, Monsieur Fraser."

The slightest hint of colour flashes on Simon Fraser's cheeks, and La Malice smirks at his discomfort. "Like I said, she displeased me so I sent her back north to her father."

Fraser is incredulous. "Do you seriously expect me to believe that a seventeen-year-old girl travelled all that distance upcountry by herself? Some of the Carrier have a different idea as to what happened. They claim the two of you went out on the lake last week, but only you came back."

La Malice jerks his knife out of its scabbard. "Bring those savages who make such false accusations to me so I may defend my honour!"

"Quiet, you fool!" barks Fraser. "We live in peace here only because Chief Kwah allows it. If they hear you talking like that, you're bound to get us all killed."

"Two go out and only one returns. Coincidentally enough, that's the same fate that befell Gilles Morel at Fort Misery, wasn't it?" John Stuart says. "You remember Fort Misery, don't you, La Malice? And Gilles Morel? You should. After all, you were the last one who saw him alive."

Fort Misery. I remember how puzzled Luc was that the cabin was abandoned and smashed up. So that's what happened, I think to myself.

"How many times do I have to tell this story?" asks La Malice. "Morel and I were gathering firewood near the mouth of the river. We walked on the ice. It cracked. He fell through. That's it."

"Then you abandoned the post," says Fraser, barely keeping his own anger in check. "Fort Misery alone should have made the Company enough money to pay for the upkeep of all our bases in New Caledonia. Instead, a good man vanishes and a productive fur trading fort is abandoned to the porcupines."

La Malice is stone-faced. "The Natives who lived there were hostile and refused to trade with me. I was alone and I feared for my life. What would you have done? And as far as Morel goes? These things happen in the *pays d'en haut*. The wilderness is a dangerous place."

"Especially for those left alone with you."

La Malice grins. "Some people are unlucky, I suppose."

"And some people have difficulty with the truth," says Stuart.

La Malice's voice drops to a whisper. "Are you calling me a liar, Monsieur Stuart? If so, we may need to have some words."

Words. It seems to me as I listen to this angry conversation that it may come to much more than words, but I know that it is not my place to say anything.

"Two people last seen in your company are missing," says Fraser coolly. "We have only your account as to why, and yours is a word I have trouble believing. Hold your tongue and mind your place, La Malice, or I will ensure that the next person to leave this post will be you, and it will be no mystery why."

Chapter 19

FRASER PUTS ME to work preparing Fort St. James for the upcoming winter. I spend hours gathering firewood, and when the salmon arrive I'm sent out in a canoe along with the Carrier to help set nets.

The arrival of the fish causes a great deal of celebration and relief. They have arrived late this year and there were fears they wouldn't come at all. The fish are the main winter food supply for both the fur traders and the Carrier, and their absence would mean almost certain famine.

The nets are hurriedly set and quickly fill with wriggling silver and red fish. Smokehouses throughout the village busily cure and dry the fish, and though our diet in the months ahead will be as monotonous as pemmican, at least we won't starve.

I find it hard to focus on my chores, my mind full of thoughts of Libby — and Louise. I know with a deep regret that I should have been back in England by now, but without the trip west I'd never have met the Métis girl, and I find it strange how her kiss still burns on my lips.

I have another worry as well. I've no idea how long I'm expected to stay in Fort St. James, but of one thing I'm certain: September is passing by, the leaves are falling, and the days are growing short and cold. There is no doubt that I'm stuck in this awful place for the winter at least. It will be another six months before I will have the chance to return to Montreal, let alone make it back to Liverpool to look for my sister.

I try to put these worries aside and go about my business, but even with all the work I'm assigned, time passes slowly until one crisp September day, two weeks after my arrival. Fraser calls me and the other clerks, Hugh Faries, John Stuart and Jules Quesnel, into his cabin, takes a bottle of rum from a crude wooden shelf, pours five small glasses and puts them down on the table beside McGillivray's letter.

"Gentlemen, it's time I shared some momentous news with you. We're on the verge of history. Three days downstream from here is a large river that I believe to be the Columbia, the very same river charted by Mackenzie in 1793. As most of you know, I informed Montreal of this two years ago, but they denied me permission to follow it, citing the need to establish proper trading relations with the local people in this region first."

The explorer passes each man a glass and I notice that Fraser's hand trembles slightly, with excitement or fear I can't tell. "As you are also aware, a shorter route to the sea is vital for our economic well-being, but we also have a much larger cause of concern; I've just learned that the American president has sent two men, Messrs. Lewis and Clark, to travel overland from the east, reach the Pacific at the mouth of the Columbia, and claim the entire watershed as their own. Such an act cannot go unchallenged. We've been charged to reaffirm British interests in the region."

Stuart slams his empty glass down onto the table. "And about time! I know your feelings towards the Americans, Simon, but they aren't our only worry. The Russians are pushing south from Alaska, and Nootka Convention or not, the Spaniards are on our doorstep as well, ready to pounce if they sense weakness. The future of the Empire in western North America may very well depend on our success."

Fraser refills the glasses. "I couldn't agree more, John, and neither could McGillivray. We leave next spring to claim this river for both Crown and Company. A toast to our success! Mackenzie believed the Columbia too turbulent to travel, but I'm confident it will lead us safely to the sea and to our fortunes. There are untold riches to be had from this land, and it's up to us to make certain they belong to the British Empire — and to us!"

Chapter 20

"IT WON'T BE LONG now until winter comes, Duncan," says Jules Quesnel, Fraser's youngest clerk and my best friend at Fort St. James. "It's barely October but we've already had frost on the ground and the leaves are quickly turning. Within three weeks we'll have our first snowfall, then for five long months it will be nothing but snow and ice.

"Before winter sets in, however, we have one important task to complete," Quesnel says. "Simon wants us to travel to the Columbia to build a small fort. He plans on befriending the people of that region, and getting as much information about the river as he can before the spring. He's been dreaming of this trip for as long as I've known him, and the news about Lewis and Clark was very unsettling. He can't stand the thought of the Americans claiming this land."

"But Mr. Fraser *is* an American," I say.

"Simon was born in New York, that's true," agrees Quesnel, "but he's a United Empire Loyalist. When he was a little boy, his father served in the British army during the war and died in an American jail. His family lost everything after the Revolution, and they fled to Montreal with the clothes on their backs and little else. Losing your home like that? That's not the sort of thing someone like Fraser forgets."

Or someone like me, I think, understanding Fraser's feelings better than anyone in the fort could possibly imagine.

Two days later, eight of us leave Stuart's Lake under Fraser's charge, canoes full of tools and other building materials. The morning chill turns my breath to an icy fog, and thick white frost blankets the dying grass along the shores.

Duyunun, Chief Kwah's main advisor, accompanies us. In his early fifties, tall and slender with long black hair flecked with grey, Duyunun knows many of the languages spoken in the region. He's been sent by Chief Kwah to translate for the Nor'Westers — and to keep us out of trouble.

Fraser and his men are on good terms with the Carrier people, or Dakelh, "the people who travel on water," as they call themselves, but they have had limited contact with others, and Duyunun's presence offers safety. Kwah is a powerful and respected chief in the region; few would dare to offend him by killing those under his protection.

"This should be an easy enough journey," says Quesnel. "Two days on tame water with no portages is my idea of canoeing."

"And no getting up at two in the morning and chewing a mouthful of pemmican fer breakfast!" I exclaim.

Quesnel agrees. "If you think pemmican's bad just wait until you live a winter on smoked salmon. It'll keep you alive, but by March you'll be willing to trade everything you have for a strip of mouldy pemmican and a bowl of cold pea soup!"

The birch and aspen trees along the mist-shrouded river are ablaze with red and yellow leaves. The air is cold and pure, and everywhere there is wildlife. In the sky, flocks of honking geese wing south for warmer climes, while beaver and otter swim in the river. Larger mammals crash through the undergrowth as well, appearing occasionally at the water's edge. Black bears and deer are common, and a few hours from the trail Lapointe and I had travelled on to reach Fort St. James, we even see a grizzly bear.

It's the largest bear I've ever seen. I look in awe as the animal noses through the shallows of the river, searching for the few remaining salmon carcasses that rot on the muddy banks. Sensing our presence, the cinnamon-coloured grizzly stands on its hind legs to get a better look. The bear must be ten feet tall, and even from the relative safety of the canoes we keep our guns at the ready. A bear that massive could easily knock down a tree or rip a man in two with its claws, and it isn't until the beast shuffles away into the brush that we breathe easy again.

An hour or so past the bear sighting, our canoes round a corner and a large clearing on the river's edge comes into view. "This looks like a good spot to set up camp," says Quesnel, pointing to the shore.

Fraser studies the opening in the woods carefully. "This is an old village site, I believe. Duyunun, do you know anything about this place?"

The Dakelh man's lips are pursed, and he has a strange fearful look in his eyes. "This is Chunlac. I wouldn't stay a night here for all the guns in the North West Company."

I shiver at his response. There is something quite eerie about the clearing. Just ten minutes ago the river had been alive with birds, jumping fish and other animals. Now it is deathly silent.

"When I was a little boy, Chunlac was a large and prosperous village," he says. "A man named Khadintel was chief here. One day when he was away hunting with his men, a band of Tsilhqot'in warriors from the south came to avenge the killing of a number of their people that had happened several years before. They spared no one. When Khadintel returned, he saw his home burned, the bodies of his family cut to pieces and the children of the village sliced open, stuck on sticks like salmon drying in the sun."

My skin prickles as Duyunun continues his story, every man listening intently. "Khadintel gathered up a band of warriors, travelled south, and the same treatment his children received was returned on the Tsilhqot'in."

"That's awful!" I say.

Duyunun shrugs. "Vengeance is the way of things," he says simply. "Don't think for a moment the Tsilhqot'in would spare you if they knew you were allied with my people. This happened when I was just a boy, but memories and hatred live a long time here. The past is a living thing."

Two hours later when Duyunun is satisfied we are far enough away from the ruined village, Fraser orders the canoes ashore. We set up camp in a small meadow, eat a cold and uneasy meal and go to bed. In the morning when the sun breaks clear of the mist, our mood lightens. Travelling is easy, and we forget about the ghosts of Chunlac.

Within the hour Stuart's River flows into a larger one. "Is this the Columbia?" I ask.

"No," says Quesnel. "Fraser hasn't named this one yet but it flows into the Columbia further downstream. We're more than halfway there. We'll reach our destination well before sunset."

Quesnel is proven right when, by late afternoon, we reach the confluence of a new, much bigger river. "Welcome to the Columbia," says Fraser triumphantly, beaching the canoes at a place not far from where the rivers meet and large cotton-wood trees line the shore. "We'll build our post here. Next spring we'll leave from this very spot and make history."

Four days of hard labour is all it takes us to build Fort

George, named in honour of our distant King. The fort is just a rough-cut log cabin made from the small pine trees abundant in New Caledonia, but it will be an adequate pushing off place for both the voyage next spring and a decent home for Hugh Faries and the two voyageurs Fraser's ordered to winter in the new fort to gather both intelligence and furs.

"Simon, when we get back to Fort St. James, you should send La Malice here as well," suggests Stuart. "I'm not looking forward to spending the winter with him. He's not taken well to young Mr. Scott, nor is he one to let grudges go."

"I'm well aware of La Malice's temperament, and that's exactly why I have to keep an eye on him."

"Are you sure that's wise? You know the sort of trouble he can brew."

"That's exactly why," says Fraser. "Hugh's a decent enough man, but he's not strong enough to endure a long winter with La Malice. Besides, I'd like to return to Fort George in the spring and find a cache of furs instead of an abandoned post and bones."

"I see," says Stuart. "This is a case of keeping your friends close . . ."

"And my enemies closer." Fraser winks at me. "Young Duncan Scott is just going to have to find a way to endure La Malice this winter. We all are."

Chapter 21

THICK CLOUDS TURN the late December skies above Fort St. James black. A strange metallic tang in the air sits right on the tip of my tongue as Quesnel and I walk through the crisp air towards the lake. "You can taste it, can't you?" says Quesnel. "The snow I mean. It's on its way and it'll be a big storm. We could be indoors for days, so let's get as much water as we can. When the blizzard hits, you won't be able to see two feet in front of your face."

We break the thin skin of ice that covers the surface of the lake near the shore to fill our water buckets. It's easy enough now to break through, but in a matter of weeks it will be thick enough to walk on.

A blast of cold air brings the snow. The first few flakes are small, hardly noticeable as we work, but within minutes larger ones fall thickly. "Hurry Duncan," Quesnel says. "We'd best get back to the cabin."

The storm hits with a fury that confines us to our cabin for two days. With the wind shrieking night and day, we live in a state of near darkness, the only light we have coming from our candles and the small fireplace.

By the afternoon of the second day the storm has blown itself out, the sun shines and, eager to shake the cobwebs from my head, I pull the door open. When I do, a small avalanche of snow slides into the cabin, followed by an intense bright light.

"Best not to be too long out there," says John Stuart, looking up from his book. "It's cold this morning."

"I just need to get out fer a little while." I have trouble finding the words to describe my restlessness. I feel edgy, as if the walls of the small log cabin are closing in on me.

"You're getting cabin fever," says Quesnel.

I've not heard the term before, but after my experience on the *Sylph*, I'm wary about illness. "Is it contagious?" I ask.

"Yes, but cabin fever's not a disease, it's a state of mind. When you're confined to quarters for an extended period of time, you can go a little funny. Some really do go insane. Stretch your legs if you want, but be careful; you may be a little tired of Stuart and me, but spending time with us is a far better option than freezing to death."

Outside, it seems as if the entire world has been whitewashed. There is still open water on the lake but it's now quite a distance farther out from shore. The air is bitterly cold, and I stamp my feet in an effort to stay warm, the snow crunching loudly beneath me, breaking the silence of the morning.

I walk down to the frozen shores of the lake. My lungs burn as I suck in the frigid air, breath rising in a steam when I exhale. It's colder than I've known before in all my seventeen years and the sensation fascinates me.

It is a remarkable landscape. Behind me is the fort and the Dakelh village of Nak'azdli. Ahead sits the grey bulk of the lake, sixty miles long, soon to be entombed in six feet of ice. On the lake's eastern shore squats Na'kal Dzulh, the Mountain of the Lake, its snow-capped peak illuminated by the first rays of the waking sun.

"It's that way to Scotland," I say, staring at the limestone-faced mountain. "That way to home." I'm so lost in my thoughts I don't hear footsteps approaching from behind.

"Enjoying the view are you, whelp?" says a familiar voice. I jump at the sound.

"La Malice, I didn't hear ye."

"Walking softly is a good skill to have in the bush."

"What do ye want?" I speak with a confidence I don't feel. The simple truth is that I'm scared of La Malice and have been since my very first day at Fort St. James.

"What do I want?" hisses La Malice, putting his arm around my neck, pulling me roughly towards him. "A little respect from you for starters."

I choke for air, flailing my arms as La Malice tightens his grasp. "I told you to be mindful out here, boy. Like I said, the wilderness is a dangerous place."

"A very dangerous place, La Malice," says Quesnel from somewhere behind me. La Malice quickly releases his grasp, and I lurch forward, gasping for breath.

"Monsieur Quesnel, how are you?" La Malice asks casually. "Out for a morning walk as well I see?"

Quesnel and Duyunun walk side by side in the snow and help me to my feet. "We both are. What were you doing?"

"Just saying hello to my old friend," says La Malice with a smile. "Now if you'll excuse me I must get back. I have a great deal of work to do."

"I do not trust him," says Duyunun, as we watch La Malice saunter back to the fort. "He has a dark soul."

I can't disagree. "Why is La Malice like that?" I ask, my breath returning to normal.

"You aren't the first to ask that question," says Quesnel. "Nobody knows where La Malice came from, and what he did before joining the Company. I don't even know his real name for that matter, but there are stories and speculation. All I know is that bad things have happened to people in his company."

"Like to Gilles Morel at Fort Misery?" I ask.

Quesnel agrees. "Fraser suspected something but there wasn't any proof. After all, 'the wilderness — '"

"' — is a dangerous place.' I've heard that before."

"On that point he's right," says Quesnel, "so make sure you're never alone with him. Fraser would let him go for sure even without evidence, but La Malice is an amazing man with the canoe. None better. And Fraser knows he will be useful once we start down the Columbia. Now let's get back to the cabin. I think you've had enough fresh air for one day, don't you?"

Chapter 22

THE LONG ICICLES that have hung from the roof since November finally start to melt. The days pass, the snow slowly disappears and trees and shrubs produce small pale green buds. Shoots of fresh grass spring up from exposed ground and the rivers and creeks appear as well, swelling in their freshet, more than one bursting its banks.

I'm splitting firewood with an axe when Fraser approaches. "Well, Mr. Scott, we are leaving for the Columbia soon. Are you still game to accompany me as McGillivray said you were?"

I'd rather go back to England, I think miserably. It's almost two years since my parents died and I left my sister behind on the Liverpool waterfront. But when I recall my conversation with McGillivray, and the poster he has locked in his desk, I know what the answer to the question must be. "Aye, I'd like to come, Sir," I say with what I hope passes for excitement.

"Then come with me you shall, Mr. Scott! We leave before the end of the month!"

We depart Fort St. James for Fort George ten days later. La Malice comes along as well. Everyone knows he thinks the mission is a fool's errand, and has made no secret sharing that opinion, but because he is such an expert with a canoe, Fraser has insisted that he accompany us.

When we arrive at Fort George, we discover to our great delight that not only have Hugh Faries and his two voyageurs survived the winter, they'd even managed to obtain some furs and make friends with the local people who have proven to be more than willing to share their knowledge of the river with Fraser. We spend the next week preparing for the journey and learning what we can about the river ahead, until finally, on the night of May 27, 1808, Fraser addresses us.

"Gentlemen, at dawn we leave on a journey that will protect the Empire, guarantee the survival of our great Company and enhance our own legacies. Sometime during the next six weeks we'll enter the Pacific Ocean at the mouth of the Columbia, and while we may encounter dangers along the way we will survive them all and be triumphant!"

The men cheer and fire their guns into the dusk sky. "Good

luck to us all!" cries Fraser. "The river and our destiny await!"

At dawn, twenty-five men in four canoes leave Fort George. It's a beautiful sunny day, and with the current slow and steady, the trip is uneventful until four hours or so to the south, when we encounter our first set of rapids.

They prove to be not too formidable, and I love the rise and fall of the canoe and the rush of cold water on my face. It's exhilarating to fly over the white water, and I could have paddled all day, but when the river slows an hour later, Fraser points towards the bank and directs the canoes into shore for us to rest.

"At least we won't starve," says La Chapelle, a short voyageur with a bushy blonde beard. "Deer spoor. There must be plenty of game around here. I'll take fresh venison any day over this damned dry fish!"

"We'll hunt when we can," agrees Fraser, "but we'll cache some of our salmon as well. It's getting a little old to be sure, but we may need it on our return."

"You mean *if* we come back," grumbles La Malice. "If the river or the savages of these parts don't kill us first."

"You worry too much, La Malice," Fraser says, pointing to a small creek that flows into the river ahead. "Do you see that stream? It is hereby named La Malice creek in your honour. Now we have to return, if only so I can put your name on the map!"

After a short rest we return to the water. Two hours later, a cluster of dwellings on a small hill above the river comes into view, reminding us that we aren't entering an empty land.

"The Nazkoten people live here," says Duyunun. "Although we are on good terms with them, protocols demand that we ask their permission to pass through their territory." Fraser agrees and we beach our canoes at the village site. "Get some trade goods from the canoe, Duncan," says Fraser, "and accompany us to the village."

Fraser, Duyunun and I walk cautiously up to the houses. Nobody seems to be about as we reach the edge of the small community. "We'll leave a blanket, a pot and some knives," says Fraser. "I can't see them, but these people are around somewhere, I know it. I'm hoping these gifts will show that we're friendly."

We place the gifts in a prominent location, return to the canoes and push out into the river. No other villages appear on the shore, and we travel without incident until a few hours further downstream when we hear the dull roar of rapids in the distance. Fraser orders the canoes beached so that we can scout the river ahead on foot. "The water's very turbulent here, Simon," says Stuart, after examining the river. "I suggest we décharge."

A décharge is a calculated risk; unladen canoes are sent through the rapids under the control of the best paddlers, while the goods are carried by the rest of the men. A décharge takes less time than a portage. It ensures the safety of the provisions, but empty or not, the precious canoes can still be damaged in the rough water.

Fraser agrees and I soon see why La Malice has been brought along, despite his temperament. "Mr. Stuart, La Malice, Baptiste and Boucher will each ride a canoe," Fraser says, "and La Malice will lead them through the cataracts. The rest of us will walk."

Plan established, the chosen paddlers push out into water. With La Malice at the front, they quickly float downstream. "Well then, men," says Fraser, "put on your tumplines, it's time to earn your pay."

"Those four are the finest paddlers in the Company, and La Malice is the best by far," says Quesnel, as I watch the canoes bob and weave through the rapids. "He'll pick a route through the torrent and keep the others safe. He may be a most unpalatable fellow, but if La Malice can't navigate a river, nobody can."

The canoes disappear and I ready my sash for the heavy load. Bales on our backs, we follow an animal track along the edge of the canyon above the river. The path is steep and slippery, and it's with great relief when, nearly nine hundred paces later, the trail leads back down to the river where we rejoin our companions who laze on a gravel bank in the afternoon sun.

"Did you get lost?" jokes Boucher as we stagger up to the canoes. "We'd have cooked dinner except you have the food!" Boucher, nicknamed Waccan, is a young, strongly built black-eyed Métis with a scraggly moustache and short black beard. Waccan is greatly respected, and slightly feared by his peers.

With his hands as adept at fighting as paddling, he has found few in the wilderness who dare cross him.

We make camp and resume our voyage early the next morning. For several days we encounter neither rapids nor people, and we travel without incident until the monotony of the river is broken by an excited shout from Fraser.

"Look to the western bank!" he yells. Not seeing what has animated our leader, we paddle towards shore. I strain my eyes but can see nothing extraordinary at all. "That tree! The one with the blaze marks on it! Do you see it?" he asks.

The tree in question is a giant grey cottonwood with a faded axe scar on its side. As we approach I see the initials "A.M." cut into its side. A small but well-travelled path heads into the bush beside it. "That's Mackenzie's mark!" Fraser exclaims. "It must have been here that he abandoned the river and headed west overland. He made his own way to the Pacific through dense forest and razor-sharp mountain ridges meant only for goats. A fantastic journey but utterly impractical. Now it's up to us to find a commercial route to the ocean and show the courage Mackenzie lacked."

"Was Mackenzie really without courage?" asks La Malice. "Or do you think the Scotsman knew something we don't?"

As we sit in our canoes on the river, a sudden movement on the trail catches my eye, and Waccan's hand slowly travels to the long knife at his belt as a man emerges from the trees. "I don't know," he replies. "But I've a feeling we're about to find out."

Chapter 23

A DOZEN MORE PEOPLE come out of the forest, waving and shouting at us. The mood in the canoes grows tense as an armed man riding a large dappled horse approaches the shore, a bow in his hand, arrow notched. "The Secwepemc people," says Duyunun. "I don't think they mean us harm but we need to be careful."

"Beach the canoes," says Fraser. "And whatever you do, take care not to make any sudden moves."

We do so, paddling cautiously until we glide up onto the shore. With knees shaking, we watch apprehensively as Fraser and Duyunun approach the waiting people, carrying with them a roll of colourful cloth and a handful of knives.

Fraser offers the gifts to the man on horseback and thanks him for allowing us passage through their country. Duyunun translates and as soon as the people are convinced we mean them no harm, the horseman dismounts, slings his long bow over his shoulders and takes the presents.

We aren't the first Nor'Westers these people have encountered. The Secwepemc remember Alexander Mackenzie. Some even guided him on his voyage, we learn, when an older man proudly shows us a knife he'd been given by the famous explorer.

"If you're following his path you need to leave the river and follow the grease trail west," says the horseman. He's very impressive: tall and strongly built with buckskin leggings and a caribou-hide robe. His bow is covered in snakeskin and the arrows that fill his quiver are straight and long and tipped with deadly sharp flint. Clearly this is not a man to anger.

"I know," says Fraser diplomatically, "but our intention is to travel down this river." Translated, his words are greeted with waves of laughter by the Secwepemc.

"There are rapids downstream that can swallow a canoe and the men within it whole," the tall man says. "If you want to go to the sea I suggest you travel overland, though I'd leave your Dakelh companion here if you want to keep your heads. His people are not held in high esteem by our Tsilhqot'in neighbours."

"I value your advice and thank you for it," replies Fraser, "but we follow this river, no matter what the risks."

The horseman shakes his head and smiles as if he were speaking to a child. "If you're determined to continue then you'll need all the help you can get. Xats'ull, our village, is just a few hours downriver. I'm sure our chief Xlo'sem will help you. I will ride ahead and let him know you are coming."

"Thank you," says Fraser. "You've been most gracious."

The man points to Gagnier, who stands leaning on his musket. "That's one of your weapons that make a great noise and smoke, isn't it? I'd like to see how such a thing works."

"It would be my pleasure," says Fraser. "Gagnier! Get the swivel gun from the canoe! Our new friends would like a demonstration of our firepower. We'll show them the biggest one we have!"

The swivel gun is something between a small cannon and a very big musket. It's too large for a man to shoulder and is fired while supported by a metal pole. It's the most powerful weapon we have, and Fraser intends to use it to full effect.

"Watch closely, Duncan," whispers Quesnel. "I've no idea how these people will react but it will be something they'll remember for the rest of their lives, I guarantee you that."

With his audience assembled, Fraser is ready to put on the show. "Now Gagnier, if you would be so kind as to shoot." Gagnier loads the weapon and aims it at a spindly pine, expecting to blow the tree to pieces, but when he pulls the trigger something goes terribly wrong. Instead of hitting its target, the barrel of the gun explodes, sending hot metal fragments whizzing through the air.

I feel a sharp, stinging pain on my face. I cry out in pain and shock and fall to my knees. I put my hand to my face and discover that my cheek is wet and sticky with warm blood where a piece of the shrapnel has cut me, but my injury is minor. I'm much more concerned for Gagnier, lying on the ground a few feet from me, his hands covering his head, blood everywhere.

I get up and rush over towards Gagnier, and am greatly relieved to discover that despite the blood he isn't seriously hurt either. Several jagged chunks of metal have cut his arms and scalp, but his wounds aren't deep and, like me, he's more shocked than injured. As the others gather around, Quesnel and I pull Gagnier to his feet, and when Stuart bandages him up, the voyageur offers profuse apologies.

"*Pardonnez-moi*! I only used a light load of powder! I have no idea why it misfired!"

"The gun was old and the barrel thin," says Fraser, relieved Gagnier is still alive. "The important thing is that no one was seriously injured. Had we hurt one of these people, the consequences might have been fatal — for us."

The horseman quickly recovers his composure, and when he speaks, the rest of his people laugh long and hard.

"What did he say?" asks a sheepish Gagnier.

"He said you should learn how to use a bow and arrow!" replies Duyunun, chuckling as well. "While your weapon sounds impressive, it isn't much good if the only people it harms are its owners!"

Chapter 24

A FEW MILES SOUTH of Mackenzie's tree, a furious stretch of water appears, much more turbulent than anything we've yet seen. Fraser orders the canoes into a calm back eddy where he takes a reading of the sun's position with his sextant.

Measurement taken, Fraser adds the stretch of the river to his oilskin map and then addresses us. "We've only travelled twelve miles since leaving our new friends, and as much as I'd like to stay on the water it seems that we must walk, for a little while at least."

The men groan but I don't mind. The day's warm but not uncomfortably so, and the scent of wildflowers and sage rises pleasantly on the warm breeze. The countryside is much different from that around Fort St. James. Grasslands have replaced the thick forests of the north, bees buzz amid the mass of flowers, and eagles and other raptors search for prey, riding the thermals high above the ground.

Tree-covered mountains aside, this place reminds me of Red River and I half expect a herd of buffalo to appear on the horizon. I think of Louise and smile, hoping someday to see her again. "That's quite a grin," says Quesnel. "It's that Métis girl you told me about, isn't it?"

"Aye." Unconsciously my hand strays to the medicine bag that Louise gave me and is now hanging around my neck.

"A medicine bag's a very special gift. You must have left quite the impression on her!" says Quesnel.

My cheeks redden and I quickly tuck the bag back under my shirt. "Louise told me to put things in it, to help me remember the trip."

"I don't know if the bag will be large enough. We've a long way to go before we reach the sea. There'll be many more memories to collect yet." My smile fades. Jules Quesnel is right. Months lie ahead before I can even contemplate returning to Red River, let alone begin my search for my sister.

But there are more pressing things to worry about right now, and one of them is the churlish voyageur with the dark beard walking alongside Waccan at the rear of the group. "He might be a good paddler but La Malice does nothing but complain," I say. "He hates me, thinks this journey is a waste of time, and he doesn't seem to care fer Mr. Fraser much either."

"He'll do his duty and keep us safe on the river — if we ever get back on it. In the meantime there are better things to occupy your thoughts. Louise, for instance, I'm sure she has a much prettier face than our grumpy voyageur!"

A few hours of walking brings us to Xats'ull, a large collection of pit houses on the edge of a plain overlooking the river. The entire community has assembled and waits expectantly for us to arrive. The horseman we'd met upstream stands beside his mount and nods as we approach.

The Secwepemc at Xats'ull are a fierce looking people, coloured with red ochre and dressed in leather leggings and deerskin robes. I'm more than a little nervous when their chief Xlo'sem, an old man with steel-grey hair, dressed in leathers and flanked by warriors, approaches.

"I travel this river to the sea," Fraser explains, "and your people told me that you would help us."

Xlo'sem motions to a middle-aged man. "My slave's from the sea. What do you want to know?"

"How long will it take to get there, and what is the river like ahead?" Fraser asks.

The man speaks, Duyunun translates, and although I don't understand a word of the response, the sour expression on the slave's face makes it quite clear that the answer won't please Simon Fraser.

"The sea is just three weeks downstream," explains Duyunun. That part of the response is met with grunts of approval; a short trip to the Pacific Ocean is a much better option than a six-month trek to Montreal.

"But only if we live to complete the journey. Not four days' travel from here, the river is alive with rapids so terrible no canoe can travel through them safely, and if we try to paddle on the water we will most certainly die."

Mutters of discontent rise from the voyageurs. "The river is the least of our worries," Duyunun continues. "The people who live along its southern reaches near the sea are called the Musqueam. They have often been invaded by warriors from the north, and now they are suspicious of any strangers. They are dangerous warriors and might either enslave us or kill us if they thought we were enemies. It was the Musqueam who stole the slave from his people then traded him up the river until he ended up here. He says he knows every inch of it between here and the sea, and that only madmen or fools would want to continue much further south."

Tensions rise, and I wonder just what Fraser will say to convince the men to continue, but before he can respond, Xlo'sem gives a long and flowing speech that draws gasps from his people, especially from the slave.

"The chief says that if we're determined to reach the sea, then he and his slave will go with us," Duyunun says in surprise. "He asks nothing in return, but wishes to have one of our guns for hunting on our return. He has influence all along the river and promises that his presence will ensure our safety."

With this proclamation, the crisis is averted. People bring us food, and we enjoy the best meal we've had in days.

While we eat, Xlo'sem holds court around the fire, chatting animatedly about the trip ahead, but the same can't be said for the slave who sits scowling in the shadows, an unhappy look on his face.

"I wonder why he's so worried?" I say. "If the river's too fast we'll just portage around it. And as fer the Musqueam — whoever they are — we've got guns. We're more than capable of looking after ourselves."

"Maybe the slave knows something else," replies Quesnel. "Perhaps it is not only the rapids or the Musqueam he fears, but something, or someone else."

Chapter 25

"DO YOUR PEOPLE travel this stretch often?" Fraser asks, eyeing the river as it constricts and froths in the narrow canyon ahead. The slave was right, I have to admit it. Although we've been on the water for only five or so hours since leaving Xats'ull, the rapids ahead are some of the roughest I've ever seen, even worse than when we had to décharge.

Xlo'sem's eyes twinkle. "No, but I can't imagine it could stop people like you." The challenge is not unexpected, and I can tell by the look on Fraser's face that he is considering ordering the canoes forward, but when he signals the brigade to the shore, it is obvious that he has chosen not to rise to the bait. For now.

Several hours of daylight remain but we're tired and wet. A

warm fire and a bowl of soup will be very welcome before tackling the rapids. Exhausted paddlers, even skilled ones, can make fatal mistakes.

Not long after we land, a small group of people appear on the canyon's edge high above the riverbank, and I watch with apprehension as the visitors make their way down the steep path towards us. "Don't worry. These are my people and they are coming to welcome us," says Xlo'sem.

The newcomers are very cordial. Gifts are exchanged and the people look at their chief with renewed respect. His people seem to think he leads our company and are pleased to see us, much to my relief — and Xlo'sem's satisfaction.

When the sun slips below the western bank, our guests take their leave, vanishing into the fading light, promising to return the next day. We post a watch but receive no night-time visitors. It isn't until a little after sunrise when I see that the chief's people have returned on the cliffs over the river, this time in even greater numbers. Word has spread, it seems, of the white men who ride the river, and many people have come to watch us.

John Stuart, Simon Fraser and I scramble up the steep slope to inspect the river ahead. From this vantage point above the river, what we see in the canyon far below fills Stuart with trepidation.

"Simon, we can't take loaded canoes through this chasm. At best we'd lose our provisions. At worst? We risk drowning the men and wrecking the boats."

"Or maybe they aim to do that themselves," says Fraser,

looking at the growing crowd just one hundred yards or so downstream. "These people seem friendly enough, but it could be an act. They could easily roll boulders onto the canoes as they pass below and smash them to pieces. It wouldn't be the first time men have been ambushed, killed and robbed in the wild by people pretending to be friends. We don't know what their true intentions may be. We carry valuable supplies after all, highly coveted by these people."

I can't help thinking that Fraser is being overly suspicious, for the people seem friendly. But then I remember Tinker and what he did to us, and I realize it is right to be cautious.

Stuart's more concerned about the dangers of the rapids. He says, "Safety is our first priority. I know you want to put on a show, Simon, to impress Xlo'sem's people, but it's madness to travel this water with fully laden canoes without testing it first. Let's send an empty canoe through with two paddlers to try the river first. If they feel it is passable then we can send the loaded canoes through."

Stuart has every right to be concerned. As far as we can see ahead the river tumbles and twists through a canyon scarcely forty yards wide, spraying white and green foam high into the air. "Do you have your pistol?" Fraser asks.

"Two," replies Stuart, "and a full bag of powder."

"Good. You and the Scott lad will stand guard over the canoe as it passes below and keep an eye on our audience."

Once Fraser has returned to camp, Stuart passes me a large flintlock pistol, a powder horn and a leather pouch. "Do you know how to shoot?" he asks.

I take a deep breath. Then, remembering Lapointe's lessons on the way to Fort William, I pour black powder down the barrel, pull a round metal ball from out of the pouch, wrap it with a small piece of fabric and tamp it down the barrel with a short metal rod.

Stuart watches approvingly as I place more of the gunpowder into a small opening on the top of the gun and cock the pistol. "Aim and fire, correct?"

"Well done, lad. Now we stand ready to protect our canoe as it passes below." As we walk towards the Secwepemc, I gaze down apprehensively as La Malice and Baptiste push out into the current.

"Keep your pistol tucked in your belt unless I tell you otherwise," warns Stuart. "If we need to protect our friends it won't be trees we're shooting at. If you aim that gun at a person then you'd better be prepared to kill."

Chapter 26

DISASTER STRIKES seconds later. The canoe enters the rapids and is quickly pulled by the current into an eddy. It spins wildly about, despite the frantic efforts of its crew to control it. Certain the canoe is about to get sucked under the surface and the men die, I turn away in horror. Even La Malice deserves a better fate than this, but when a cheer arises from the spectators I look back to the river to see that somehow our companions have been spit out of the vortex.

The canoe continues helter-skelter on its way until Baptiste and La Malice miraculously regain control and manage to force it onto a large flat rock where they stop, clinging precariously to the edge of the canyon wall.

From far below I hear Fraser shout. "Mr. Quesnel! Rope! Quickly!" I watch as Quesnel takes a length of rope from a canoe then follows Fraser up the path. There is no riverbank here. Quesnel and Fraser must climb to the top of the canyon, to a point overlooking the rock, where Baptiste and La Malice wait anxiously for help.

Finally in position at the top, Fraser ties the rope to a stout pine tree, throws it over the cliff and then, holding onto the rope, gingerly descends the soft clay bank towards the men. At the bottom he secures the canoe with the rope, then, holding onto the rope again and using his knife to cut foot and handholds into the clay, leads Baptiste and La Malice slowly back to the top.

The trio inch their way up, and when the exhausted Nor'Westers pull themselves over the edge to the safety of the path, I breathe a deep sigh of relief. The Secwepemc people on the banks break out in wild applause, clearly as pleased as I that our men have survived.

Fraser faces his audience, bows politely as if he'd put on the show just to please them, then he and Quesnel carefully pull the light birchbark canoe up the cliff to safety.

"This stretch of the river is impassable," says Stuart. "I can't imagine that Simon will be very happy with today's events."

We return to camp, and just as Stuart predicted, Fraser is upset. But Simon Fraser isn't the only man angry with the day's events. La Malice and Baptiste warm up by the fire, wrapped in woollen blankets whispering angrily to each other. "That one is up to something," says Stuart. "We'll have to watch him like a hawk."

A few hours later, a Secwepemc man approaches. After the near disaster, we're on edge, but the fellow is friendly enough and makes a surprising offer. "The water's too dangerous to travel on," he says. "Leave your canoes here and we'll look after them. We have horses and you may borrow some to help you carry your belongings. The Nlaka'pamux people live downriver. They are our friends and will almost certainly give you canoes when you reach them."

Fraser is polite but noncommittal. "Thank you very much for your generous offer. My men and I will consider it and give you our answer in the morning." Fraser bids him farewell and disappears into his tent with John Stuart in tow.

"This will be an interesting night," says Quesnel. "It's only been eleven days since we left Fort George, and Simon won't be willing to abandon the Columbia. After all, he's staked his reputation on this river. Dangers or not, it's going to take a very powerful argument from Stuart to make him change his mind."

Chapter 27

I SHAKE OFF THE early morning chill and join the voyageurs who huddle sullenly around the fire. "Eat as much soup as you can," says D'Alaire. "You're going to need all your strength today, I'd wager."

"What are ye talking about?" I ask.

"I overheard Fraser and Stuart talking early this morning," he says. "Fraser's going to accept the offer of horses to help carry our things, but he's decided he can't trust these people with our canoes so we'll be packing them up that cliff and carrying them on our backs for days, no doubt."

As if on cue, Fraser emerges from his tent. "Gather round, men, I need to speak to you." He chooses his words slowly and carefully. "As you know, these people have agreed to lend us some horses, but it will also be necessary to bring the canoes since we simply can't count on finding any downstream."

"I told you," whispers D'Alaire.

La Malice is defiant. "And what if we refuse to continue, Monsieur? I nearly drowned yesterday on this fool's mission."

The men fall silent. It's exceptionally rare for a voyageur to question a clerk, let alone someone of Fraser's rank. The tension escalates as we wait for a response.

Fraser clenches his jaw but maintains his composure. "You could leave if you want, La Malice, but you have been hired by the North West Company to do a job so I suggest you see it through." Fraser's hand moves deliberately towards his pistol. Instinctively I edge towards Fraser, my own hand inching closer to the knife in my belt.

"You're not about to disobey the orders of your superior, are you, La Malice?" asks Fraser coldly, his eyes glaring at the voyageur. "If you did, I'd be within my rights to shoot you on the spot." The two men face each other, neither prepared to give an inch. After what seems an eternity, La Malice speaks.

"You're right, of course, Monsieur. Nobody here is a coward, least of all me. It seems we'll reach your precious ocean or die trying."

La Malice brushes roughly past me. "I saw your hand stray to your belt. Thinking of putting a blade in me were you, whelp? Best keep that knife handy then if I was you — you're apt to need it before this trip is through."

I try to put La Malice's threat out of my mind when, an hour or so later, the Secwepemc reappear and lead four horses down the steep track to the riverbank. We load the animals with supplies, then prepare to lead them back up the steep track.

Following Fraser, I take the first horse. Moving slowly and deliberately, I almost reach the top of the canyon when, without warning, the trail gives way under the horse's hooves. The animal slips, and for a second its weight nearly pulls me off my feet. I grasp the leather strap and hold tight, fighting my own panic as the horse's bulk drags it towards the edge of the path.

As the animal's hooves flail wildly, it whinnies in terror, but just as it is about to fall to its death, the strap holding the bales breaks. Our supplies fall from the horse's back and plummet down the cliff face, bouncing off the rocks and into the river, disappearing in the turbulent water far below.

Relieved of the weight, the animal recovers its balance, and with eyes white with fright, sprints up the rest of the path, pulling the harness from my hands. "What did we lose?" yells Fraser from the top of the cliff as the horse hurtles past him, disappearing in the scrub.

"At least half of our dried salmon and most of our medical equipment!" Stuart shouts up. Fraser curses at the news. The loss of the gear, especially the medicine, is a great blow. The journey can continue without them, but the accident and Fraser's next command do nothing to ease the mood amongst the men.

"Unload the other horses," he orders. "They can carry our things along the trail, but we can't trust them on this hill. We'll have to pack the gear up from the river ourselves."

"Are you certain, Simon?" asks Stuart. "This won't make the men happy. A regular portage is one thing but carrying bales on your back up this slope is something else altogether."

Fraser is resolute. "I don't like it either, John, but we can't afford to lose anything else. The men know their roles. Make the order."

The voyageurs react with disapproval at the command, but Waccan silences them with a hard stare, picks up the heaviest bale himself and starts up the path. The others follow and within two hours all the bales and our canoes are safely at the top.

The sunset is beautiful, caressing the western sky with long crimson and orange streaks, but almost none of the exhausted men stay awake to appreciate it. As soon as we eat our meal of cold dried salmon we unroll our blankets and fall asleep. Tomorrow, we know, will be a difficult day.

Chapter 28

AS DAWN BREAKS, Fraser, Stuart, Quesnel and I leave camp and the grumblings of the men behind to scout conditions ahead. The path twists up and down the hills along the roof of the canyon. Even at this early hour, the heat bounces off the ground, making travelling difficult, and I can only imagine how much harder it will be loaded down with gear and canoes.

As we walk I see something move quickly in the brown grass in front of Fraser. "Simon!" I cry. "By your feet! Look out!"

With reflexes hardened by his years in the bush, Fraser leaps backwards, falling awkwardly. Stuart pulls out his pistol and fires at a spot on the ground just two yards in front of Fraser, the shot echoing off the rocks.

"Did it get you?" Stuart asks.

Fraser hurriedly inspects his feet and legs. "I don't think so." The "it" in question is a large, light-coloured snake with dark splotches along the length of its thick body. Not quite dead from Stuart's bullet, the bleeding reptile twists back and forth on the ground, a strange rattling sound coming from the horned segments at the end of its tail.

"You're lucky the boy saw it," says Stuart, picking up a heavy stick and clubbing the writhing snake until it lies still. "That rattlesnake could have killed you had you taken another step."

"Not so lucky, blast it all!" curses Fraser. Although he's avoided a bite, he's banged his leg on the edge of sharp rock when he fell, and blood drips freely from the nasty gash. "And of course our bandages fell into the river because of that cursed horse!"

Fraser tries to stand but I see that his leg is hurting him. He slumps back down. "It seems that we've no choice but to remain here for the day; I'm in no shape for a hike now." For the first time in the voyage Fraser looks defeated.

"Simon, why don't Jules, Duncan and I scout ahead anyway?" suggests Stuart, looking to take something positive away from the turn of events. "We'll help you back to camp and then carry on. We should soon be able to judge whether to leave the canoes here or not. If the river's as impossible as these people say, there's no point in taking them any further.

Besides, morale's slipping amongst the men and we need to be mindful of that."

Stuart's idea is sound, and Fraser reluctantly agrees to it. "Take Duyunun, Xlo'sem and his slave. You never know whom you'll meet out here."

We return to camp with the injured explorer. Then, with Duyunun and our guides in front, we set off along the path. Far below, the river foams and roils between the arches and columns of stone that rise gracefully above the brown water. Our leader still refers to the river as the Columbia although the men have recently dubbed it Fraser's River — a name more and more fitting as the days pass.

We soon learn that paddling further won't be an option for some time to come. Here, the river's nothing but a cauldron of impassable rapids, even wilder than the stretch of water that nearly drowned La Malice.

"People!" says Duyunun suddenly.

"Where?" asks Stuart, reaching for his pistol. "I don't see anyone."

"Two men beside the tree that sticks out over the cliff. Do you see?" Duyunun's eyes are sharp. The tree in question is three hundred yards or more down the path. Not until we walk another fifty yards am I able to make out two indistinct shapes in the distance.

"It's not wise for all of us to continue," says Duyunun. "If they feel threatened it could cause problems."

"You and I will go," says Stuart. "The chief and his slave as well since they speak the language." Decision made, the four travellers set off towards the strangers. Quesnel and I remain, watching as the two groups meet and talk, amicably as far as I can tell. After a few moments Xlo'sem, his slave and Duyunun walk away with the strangers while Stuart returns alone.

"They are the Nlaka'pamux," says Stuart. The Secwepemc told us about them and that they are friends with Chief Xlo'sem. "They have invited him back to their camp, but the three of us are to return to Fraser for now. They say it would be too great a shock for all of us to arrive at their village unannounced, and they need a day or two to prepare their people for our arrival. They've asked us to wait here until they return."

Tired and dusty, we go back to camp and share all that we've seen. To no one's surprise, the injured Fraser grouses at our news, having hoped the river would get better. He's also unhappy our guides and translators have gone on ahead, leaving us completely unable to communicate with anyone we may meet.

"Construct shelters for the canoes," says Fraser. "We'll leave them here and cache some food and supplies as well. It seems that if we're to travel on the river again, it will be because of the generosity of those we meet downstream."

Waccan, La Malice and I are put to work building a pine bough covering for the canoes. "Fraser's pushing his luck this time," says La Malice, not seeming to care that I hear every word he says. "If he expects me to walk to the ocean he's crazy. I'll desert before I do that."

"Keep your voice down, you fool," says Waccan. "If you desert you can forget about ever working for the Company again. Besides, if we do survive, there's bound to be bonus pay."

"Bah! You're as bad as these clerks!" he spits. "A dead man's share of nothing is all you'll get if you stay with them. I'm leaving when I get my chance."

Then La Malice stares at me in a way that makes my blood run cold. "And if any of you try to stop me, it will be your last mistake."

Chapter 29

MY THIRST IS OPPRESSIVE. By mid-afternoon of the next day with Stuart and Duyunun still not back, most of our waterskins are empty. We'd expected to encounter many streams, but this arid stretch is utterly devoid of water save for the river, totally unreachable at the bottom of the canyon, far too steep to descend. "Drink," says Quesnel, passing his own nearly empty waterskin to me.

"Nae," I croak through my scorched throat, "I can't."

Quesnel is firm. "We're certain to find water soon but if you get heatstroke or dehydrate you'll slow us all down."

I drink gratefully, never knowing water to taste so good, as it does now. "Thank ye, Jules," I say, as the last drops slide down my throat. "I should have saved mine."

"Yes, but you've learned a valuable lesson, and you don't need an 'I told you so.'"

"Water! Only ten minutes up the path!" shouts Waccan, as if on cue. He has been scouting ahead, looking for streams and has just returned.

We quickly follow the voyageur. "Ten yards off the path by those bushes! Do you see?" We hurry to the thicket, longing for a cool drink. What we find, however, isn't fresh water at all, but a noxious pool of a white sulphureous liquid bubbling unappetizingly from the ground. One of the horses sniffs it and snorts in distaste. The animals are as thirsty as we are but they refuse to drink from the pond.

"Don't touch it," orders Fraser, limping to catch up. "That water's not safe."

"Perhaps if we dig nearby we'll find fresh water," suggests Jules.

"I doubt that very much," says La Malice, "but what do we have to lose?" Waccan digs a hole and water seeps into the hole, but it smells almost as foul as the pond next to it.

One of the other voyageurs, La Certe, pushes his way past me and throws himself onto the ground. Half-crazed by thirst, he cups his hands and drinks deeply. Almost instantly La Certe's face turns white. He spits out the rank water and rolls on the ground, retching and wailing in agony. "*Aidez-moi*! It burns!" he screams.

"People!" The cry from Quesnel turns our attention away from our suffering colleague towards the group of people, ten or so, approaching from the south.

Then we see Duyunun, and his reassuring voice cries out. "Don't worry! The Nlaka'pamux have come to bring you back to their village!"

One of the men who arrives with our friend gives La Certe a waterskin. He gulps deeply, the cool clear water rolling down his face, soaking his shirt. "Why would you drink this when there's a creek of good water just to the south of here?"

The man is tiny, almost as short as Tinker, but unlike the treacherous peddler he's young and honest-looking, with a mischievous twinkle in his eye. The village is ready for us, we're told.

Forty-five minutes later we find the promised stream, flowing clear and cold. We drink deeply, fill our own water-skins and then, refreshed, we continue on our way, stopping shortly before sunset to set up camp. The Nlaka'pamux camp alongside us and have brought us some fresh fish for dinner. I am exhausted, and warm from the fire, I am soon almost asleep with a belly full of fresh salmon. Then I hear Quesnel whispering, "What do you think those two are up to?" The slave and the chief have moved away from the others and talk quietly at the edge of the firelight.

"Who cares," I grunt. I am ready for sleep and don't care much about our guides.

When we rise in the morning we find that Xlo'sem and his slave have gone. "They left in the middle of the night," says the Nlaka'pamux man we have dubbed Little Fellow. "They had business back home they said, but wanted you to know that you are most welcome to stay with them on your return."

"Business like staying alive, I'd wager," La Malice hisses as we pack up our things. "They must know something we don't. I don't like the thought of travelling through country even a chief is scared of."

For once, La Malice is right. It is very odd that Xlo'sem would leave us, especially after promising to accompany us to the coast with the slave as our guide. It is difficult to read these people's intentions, and Fraser just shakes his head when he hears what has happened.

Because Fraser's leg still bothers him, we traverse slowly along a rough track, carved through wild country high above the river. Always in sight but impossible to approach, the river flows deep and furious within the iron walls of the deep canyon, impassable as ever. Although he speaks little of it, I know that Fraser's disappointment is growing, as is the dissent among the men. They walk, sullenly, in little knots of twos and threes, muttering to each other, casting dark glances at Fraser, and at us.

We walk all day, pausing only to refill our waterskins at the few small creeks that tumble down from the mountains. As the sun sets behind rapidly thickening clouds we stop to set up camp. "Our new companions have been very gracious," says Fraser, "but we'll find out just how friendly they really are when we reach their village tomorrow."

I wake to the steady patter of rain on my blanket. I shake off the morning cold, shivering in the damp air. Fog shrouds the mountains and canyon walls. It's the coldest it has been since leaving Fort George. By late afternoon, however, the weather clears. Streams of pale sunlight cut through the clouds, revealing a settlement sitting high on a bluff above the junction of two rivers.

The river we've been following runs fast, brown and heavy with silt. The new one, however, sparkles silver and green in the waning sun.

We arrive at the village and are quickly surrounded by hundreds of smiling men, women and children. Delicious smelling food roasts on the many campfires, and once we are settled down, I am soon able to dip into the huge wooden bowls with my hands until I'm stuffed. "This is fantastic," I exclaim, my mouth full of a fish that Duyunun calls sturgeon.

Fraser is cautious in his response. "I must admit it's nice to be treated like this, lad, but I'll reserve judgment on these people until later. Those who wear the brightest smiles sometimes carry the sharpest knives." Despite Fraser's initial suspicions, it's apparent we are guests of honour. We soon relax, feeling safe in the company of our hosts.

The evening sun hangs low above the western mountains as the large moon climbs into the sky. Fires blaze brightly, and the people of the village assemble in anticipation of the celebration to come. When everyone is seated, the Grand Chief stands and raises his hand.

The crowd falls silent. He's a tall noble-looking man, dressed in fine leathers and a large feather headdress. When he speaks, his resonant voice echoes across the plain.

"I am Tcexe'x, chief of the Nlaka'pamux people," he proclaims. "Since the world began we have lived here at this place called Kumsheen. You are welcome guests." Fraser stands and acknowledges the greeting to the cheers of the villagers.

"I've been told you travel to the sea, ten days to the south," Tcexe'x continues. "We will help you on your journey. The river and the people who live on its southern shores are dangerous. They have had tribes from the north coming by sea to take their people as slaves, and they do not welcome strangers. Still, if it is your destiny to go to the great salt water then go you will, but you will soon realize that you are better off here amongst the Nlaka'pamux!"

The crowd cheers once more, drums play and a song rises up. But not everyone celebrates. Excusing themselves from the festivities, John Stuart and Simon Fraser step away from the glow of the bonfire. The sun has set and stars twinkle brightly above, allowing Stuart to take a reading of our position, something I know he's been trying to do for the last forty-eight hours, without much cooperation from the weather.

I watch Stuart examine his sextant as if it were broken and then he reads the stars again. He turns to Fraser who takes the instrument and makes a measurement himself before shaking his head and returning it to Stuart.

The two sit in the moonlight, heads together, talking animatedly to each other. Though I can't hear his whispered words, the worried look on Simon Fraser's face tells me that something isn't right — not right at all.

Chapter 30

KUMSHEEN BUZZES WITH the news that Little Fellow and Tcexe'x himself will accompany us on the next leg of our voyage. They have heard that Xlo'sem and his slave have turned back, and perhaps they mean to show that they are much braver. No one is sure, but we welcome their offer. The water here is rough but navigable and we expect to borrow canoes and return to the river, so when Fraser orders us to leave on foot and without the horses, I'm confused.

"Jules, why aren't we on the water? These people have lots of canoes they could lend us. The river's fast, but it's still manageable."

"Downstream the river's worse than ever, apparently," he

says. "The Nlaka'pamux aren't prepared to risk their canoes, even for us. But it's not all bad news. Little Fellow promises we'll be able to get some on the other side of the rapids, and from there the river is manageable all the way to the sea."

"Do we at least know what the path ahead is like?" I ask.

"Simon asked that question as well. All he got were smiles and orders to leave the horses behind. But it can't be worse than what we've already been through, can it?"

I look at Fraser and Stuart, walking apart from the rest of us, talking quietly. "What's going on, Jules?" I ask. "I saw the two of them together last night, and it seemed that something was bothering them."

Jules Quesnel looks as glum as Fraser. "I can't talk about it right now, Duncan, but Simon will bring it up when he feels it's the right time."

I press for more information, looking for anything to explain the looks on Fraser and Stuart's faces, but despite some gentle pressure, my friend refuses to say anything more. When the rain starts falling again I'm forced to put the mystery aside and concentrate on the walk.

The razor-thin path is as slick as ice. Travelling with the heavy packs is nearly impossible, but it's our only option. The river, seething and bubbling below, is utterly impassable.

Rain falls steadily throughout the day until, wet and exhausted, we gratefully arrive at a small Nlaka'pamux settlement. The villagers feed us a meal of cold smoked fish and hazelnuts, and after dinner under clearing skies, Fraser gives a small bolt of calico cloth to our hosts. "They seem quite well off here," I say. "I'm not so sure they need anything of ours."

Quesnel agrees. "Judging by the number of pots and other metal things here, they've dealt with Europeans before."

"There's more proof of that than just pots," says Stuart sombrely. "Smallpox. Look at their bodies." The faces and arms of many of the residents are horribly disfigured with scars and pockmarks, evidence of the destructive nature of the disease.

"Europeans introduced the disease. For every one of these people who survived the pox, more than twenty died," Stuart says. The disease was introduced by European explorers and traders coming in from the Pacific and it has travelled up the canyon with tribes travelling from the south. "I don't think our presence bodes well for these people."

When we make camp, Tcexe'x informs Fraser he will return to Kumsheen in the morning. "Don't worry," the chief says, seeing the concerned looks on our faces. "The one you call Little Fellow will keep you safe."

The rains continues to fall as Tcexe'x prepares to depart the next morning. Before he does, Fraser steps forward and pins a metal broach onto the chief's deerskin vest. "You're a noble man, a great leader, and I would be honoured to give you this silver badge as a token of our gratitude," he says. "It's a strawberry flower, the symbol of my clan. I hope you remember me by it."

The chief hugs Fraser in return. "You are welcome to stay

with us for as long as you wish when you return. Be wary of the river and even more so of the Musqueam. You may not find them as welcoming as my people."

Chapter 31

WE'VE BARELY WALKED an hour when the trail disappears altogether. "Little Fellow," says Fraser anxiously, "where has the path gone?"

Little Fellow indicates a faint cut up the side of the hill, a passageway so narrow that even the keen eyes of Waccan failed to see it. "Now we go up."

Staring up the cliff face I realize why the horses weren't brought along. No one moves towards the path. Instead we stand, frozen like statues. La Malice spits contemptuously onto the ground, his eyes locked on Fraser.

Still limping from the incident with the rattlesnake, Fraser steps resolutely towards the cliff. "I don't like it either, but we won't get to the sea by stopping here." Not waiting to see if the men follow, Fraser turns and walks slowly up the narrow trail.

"You heard him," says Waccan. Slowly, reluctantly, the voyageurs follow, pressing their bodies into the rock face, shuffling slowly forward along the precarious track.

As I climb, the wind and rain whip at my body, threatening to tear me from the cliff and throw me to the water, now far below. As the rain falls I have a sudden flash of memory, back to the *Sylph* and the storm that killed Francis. I shudder at the thought.

I've never liked heights, and to make matters worse, I've somehow found myself right in front of La Malice. "Look down, whelp, and tell me you're not afraid," he says, an evil smile on his face.

Despite my fear I glance down to the river, a shimmering silver ribbon far beneath me, and I feel my legs buckle. I jam myself hard against the wall of the cliff and stand there, frozen in fear until I force myself to continue, inch by frightening inch.

Just when I think things can't get any worse, I discover that the path has completely eroded away. In its place, crude bridges of tree boughs have been placed across the gulf, allowing only the very brave — or the very foolish — to continue.

Little Fellow does his best to reassure us. "Don't worry,"

Duyunun translates. "This trail is heavily used and the bridges are repaired from time to time."

"How often is 'from time to time'?" I ask, not really wanting to know the answer.

"When someone steps on a branch and it breaks, we replace it. Now shall we continue, or do you want to turn back to Kumsheen?" Without another word, Little Fellow steps nimbly out onto the bridge and crosses over in a matter of seconds. Safe on the other side, he faces the rest of us expectantly.

"Men," says Fraser, "the Pacific Ocean is on the other side of that bridge. If I have to cross over this chasm to reach it, then so be it; I'll not turn back now to spend the rest of my life wishing that I'd had the courage to continue. I've never seen the equal to this country. It seems we have to pass where no man should venture, but pass we shall — if not for the British Empire or the Company then for ourselves."

Fraser steps out onto the bridge. It sways beneath his weight, and he stumbles slightly, but quickly recovers his balance and continues slowly until he reaches the other side.

Jules Quesnel crosses without incident, as does Stuart, Waccan, Bourbonnais and Gagnier. Then it's my turn. Swallowing the fear that rises in my throat, I step onto the bridge. The branches sag and groan, and for a heart-stopping second I'm convinced they will snap.

I press my body hard into the side of the cliff, dig my fingers into the rocks and stand like a statue, suspended hundreds of feet above the river, nothing but dead branches between me and the raging water far below. "You can do it!" shouts Gagnier.

La Malice is less encouraging. "Yes, whelp, you can fall and smash yourself into little pieces." Gathering my courage, and trying to block out La Malice's words, I take one small step across the void, desperate to feel solid ground beneath my feet.

I see a flash of movement from the corner of my eye. At first I think it's a small bird, a swallow perhaps, startled by my presence, flying out of a nest, but with a rush of fright I realize that birds don't have fingers, fingers attached to La Malice's outstretched arm, fingers that clutch strongly onto my shirt and tug.

I lose my balance and my arms fly wildly, desperately trying to find something, anything to hold. Without the weight of my pack, perhaps I would have been able to steady myself, but the heavy bale on my back pulls me, as if in slow motion, to the edge of the ramshackle bridge, and into the empty air beyond.

Chapter 32

I MANAGE TO GRAB hold of the bridge as I fall, crying in pain as my body jars to a stop, my arm feeling as if it were being pulled from my body. My pack slips from my shoulders and spirals downward through the air, exploding open on the rocks below, scattering its contents into the churning water. "Help!" I scream, my fingers and joints burning as I desperately hold onto the sagging branch.

"Don't move!" shouts Gagnier from the other side of the bridge. "I'm coming." Gagnier lies down on the path, stretches out his arm and wraps his strong hand around my right wrist. "*Bon*. Now, at the count of three let go of the branch so I can pull you up. Do you understand?"

"Let go? Are ye mad?" I cry. "I'll fall!"

"No you won't," he says. "I have your other arm. I'll pull you to safety. I swear by Sainte Anne I will." After a few seconds of hesitation, I nod.

"One," the voyageur counts as Fraser and the others watch anxiously. "Two." I exhale and then hold my breath as Gagnier tightens his grip while Bourbonnais and Waccan brace his legs; it would do no good if he fell to his death trying to save me.

"Three!" Gagnier tenses his muscles and lifts me up. I shut my eyes and let go of the wood. Gagnier's hand, made strong from years of paddling, is the only thing keeping me alive. For a few seconds I dangle in the air until Gagnier deposits me safely on the narrow path.

Never in my life have I felt so relieved. "Thank ye," I say with a shaking voice, tears of fear and relief streaming down my face. "I'll never be able to repay ye."

"I owe you, remember? You were the first to come to my assistance when that swivel gun exploded. And you!" Gagnier says angrily to La Malice. "I saw your hand on the boy's shoulder right before he slipped, I swear it!"

"Of course my hand was there," says La Malice smoothly. "I saw the boy stumble, I reached out and tried to steady him but it happened too fast. There was nothing I could do."

"Is that true, Duncan?" asks Stuart suspiciously. I don't know what to say. There's no doubt I saw La Malice's hand on my shirt, but my mind is a fog. The details are blurry and I don't know for certain whether to believe La Malice or the sickening feeling in my gut that I've almost been murdered.

"I . . . think maybe that La Malice was trying to help," I say.

A malevolent smile creases La Malice's face as he crosses the bridge without incident. "You were very lucky not to fall," he says to me, his tone sounding very much like disappointment.

There are several more bridges to cross but none quite as frightening. After another hour of travel, the path leads back down to the river at a place Little Fellow calls Spuzzum. "Are you sure about La Malice?" asks Quesnel as we descend. "Helping isn't in his nature."

"A dinnae ken fer sure, Jules. It all happened so fast."

"Well, you're very charitable to give that man the benefit of the doubt," says Quesnel, "but if I were you I'd never turn your back on him again. To murder a comrade in cold blood seems hard to believe, but keep your eyes on him and your hand on the butt of your pistol. Don't forget, more than one person has died in La Malice's company."

Chapter 33

THE PATH LEADS AWAY from the river, and we walk through forests full of huge fir trees with thick gnarled bark and aromatic cedars that tower skyward, their trunks as wide as five men.

The undergrowth is moist and dense with sword ferns, salal, and brambles that thickly carpet the forest floor. The woods are primordial and eerily quiet. With the exception of the footpath, we see no signs of human presence at all, until I smell something terrible. "Och! What's that?" I ask, my stomach heaving as a terrible stench envelops me.

Duyunun stares into the forest. "Death." Several yards off the path something that looks like a large bird's nest sits high off the ground in the branches of a large fir, but no nest I've ever seen has had a decomposing arm hanging out of it.

Something, a bird perhaps, has pulled the limb out and it hangs limply, flesh drooping in tatters off the bone. Duyunun explains that the people here bury their dead in trees or on top of mortuary poles. The superstitious voyageurs cross themselves and mutter prayers as we walk quickly past the corpse. Sainte Anne is a long way away, but with a bit of luck she can still hear us.

There are no more bodies, and soon afterwards the path leads out of the woods and back to the river. The rapids are gone and I stare longingly at the slow brown water, wishing we'd been able to bring the canoes. "We're not alone," says Fraser, pointing to smoke curling lazily into the sky ahead.

"They are the Sto:lo," says Little Fellow. "We aren't at war with them at present but be on your guard. They are not the Musqueam but they have heard of what the whites have done to their people in the south."

We reach the edge of a large village full of huge cedar houses, guarded by intricately carved posts and painted vivid reds and dark blacks.

A dozen warriors walk quickly towards us, and I stare warily at the impressive number of bows, spears and clubs they carry. "I suspect they've used their weapons to kill more than animals," Quesnel says. "We must heed Little Fellow's words and be careful."

Surrounded by armed warriors, the chief of the village

greets us cautiously. "You are the first Whites to visit us from up the river, but we know all about your people. What do you want?"

"We're travelling to the sea. We would like to purchase some canoes from you," says Fraser, waiting for Little Fellow and Duyunun to translate. To our dismay, however, the Sto:lo prove to be quite reluctant to part with their boats.

The canoes are huge and very valuable crafts, made from the hollowed trunks of trees. It would have taken a great amount of effort and time to make them, and I understand their reluctance to trade them for the few cheap pots and buttons we still possess.

After much negotiation, an agreement is reached, although Fraser isn't happy about it. The Sto:lo agree to lend us one canoe at the cost of almost all our remaining goods, but only on the condition that some of their people come along to keep an eye on the dugout craft.

Deal done, the Sto:lo return to their homes. We're not invited to dinner, so we set up camp on the outskirts of the village. We eat a sparse meal of half-rotted salmon. As night falls we set a watch and huddle around the fire, cold, hungry and nervous. When sleep finally comes, it is fitful and short as we anxiously wait for dawn.

Chapter 34

JUDGING BY THE warriors who stand between us and the canoe, their spears pointed, bows at the ready, the chief has changed his mind about lending us it. Things escalate when one of the Sto:lo takes a jacket belonging to La Malice from the top of our pile of gear and waves it triumphantly to his friends, as if it were a trophy. Before anyone can stop him, the dark-bearded voyageur tackles the thief and points his pistol at his chest. "That's mine!" he yells. "I'll kill you for that!"

Fraser is horrified. "La Malice! Stop! We're dead men if you shoot. Protect the canoe and the gear, but don't pull that trigger!" Reluctantly, La Malice steps back, allowing the warrior to scramble to his feet, forgetting all about the jacket.

We walk towards the canoe in a semi-circle, our pistols aimed at the warriors. "You promised we could borrow this canoe. I took you at your word," says Fraser. "Where I come from a man stands by his obligations."

Little Fellow and Duyunun quickly translate, and with two dozen guns aimed at him, the chief takes the opportunity to reconsider the situation. "The canoe is yours," he says sourly, to a howl of protest from his warriors.

"To borrow," he adds, brushing aside the complaints of his men. "The Musqueam are fierce warriors and may kill you, but if you survive you'll give the canoe back and leave our land forever." Decision made, the chief leaves the riverbank with his upset people following.

"You must go on without me," Little Fellow says. "I'll stay here and await your return. There's bad blood between my people and the Musqueam. My presence would only endanger you."

Fraser clasps the small man's hand warmly. "In that case we'll be back shortly," he promises. "Please be careful while we're gone. I don't trust these people."

As soon as we push out into the river, the long, heavy dugout moves quickly downstream away from the Sto:lo village. "Those are strange-looking otters," says D'Alaire a short while later, looking at several black creatures poking their whiskered noses out of the water.

"Those aren't otters," exclaims Gagnier. "They're seals! We must be nearly at the sea!" Our excitement at almost reaching our destination is short-lived. Our supply of salmon is gone. What hasn't been eaten is completely rotted. With no friendly locals to feed us, we have little choice but to make camp and scrounge for berries and shellfish along the riverbank.

Night falls. We light a fire, post guards, and while the men prepare for bed, Stuart comes up to me. "Simon would like to talk to you and Jules. Quietly," he adds.

Together we walk down the beach. When we have gone a short distance from the camp, Quesnel and I watch in silence as Stuart checks his sextant against the stars several times.

"Simon, we're still more than two hundred miles north of the known latitude of the Columbia's mouth," he says finally, "but the ocean can't be more than a few hours away. It's time to admit that —"

Fraser completes Stuart's sentence. "That we've been risking our lives on the wrong river for weeks? The stars don't lie and so I'm left with two inescapable conclusions: this is not the Columbia and I'm a failure on a grand scale. I wonder what Mackenzie will say when he hears this story."

Confused, I look at Quesnel. "The wrong river?" I ask. Quesnel nods, and then I understand. Since Kumsheen at least, Fraser and Stuart have suspected this, an outcome confirmed today with the last measurement.

"Sir, this may not be the Columbia," I tell Fraser, trying to cheer him up, "but this is still an historic discovery. Ye've found a new river and followed it from the heart of the wilderness to the sea. Even if we have walked part of the way. Who knows what the Company may do with it? They could ferry furs and supplies fer some of the trip and transfer the rest by horse."

"Going indirectly was not the object of our undertaking, Mr. Scott," replies Fraser dejectedly. "I'd hardly consider this river any good for trade. Besides, how does it help the Empire if the Americans are sitting unmolested on the banks of the real Columbia, far to the south? We've failed in both our missions."

"When will you tell the men?" asks Stuart. "They won't be pleased, but they still must be told."

Fraser reluctantly agrees. "Tomorrow, I suppose. We'll stay on course until we reach the Pacific, then return to Fort St. James immediately afterward so I can report our failure to Montreal."

"I just hope we'll be able to send word to McGillivray," Stuart says. "We've yet to run into these Musqueam. If they're as dangerous as everyone says, I'll consider this voyage a success if we make it back alive, no matter what river this may be."

Chapter 35

A LARGE OPEN GULF appears in the distance, shimmering silver in the mid-morning sun. "The sea!" shouts Waccan from the bow of the canoe. A large land mass, an island perhaps, looms in the west while to the north large snow-capped mountains, almost impressive as the Rockies, rise high into the blue sky.

"I don't see an American fort. Maybe we got here first," Gagnier says. I know that Fraser will have to tell the men the truth very soon, and I'm nervous about the outcome.

"They may not be Americans, but someone else is here," Waccan says. "Look to the northern bank." On the shore is a cluster of buildings in a grove of towering cedar trees. There is no one visible but smoke from a campfire curls lazily into the trees.

"It must be a Musqueam village," says Fraser. "We'll land and introduce ourselves before we go any further."

The idea does not sit well with La Malice. "Are you insane? You've heard what these people are like; they'll treat us as invaders. They are likely to shoot first. We need to show them that we can't be intimidated."

Fraser snaps back. "Our safety lies in openness, not skulking around like thieves. We'll greet these people as if we're guests." Remembering how I felt about the English invasion of Scotland, I can't help thinking that the Musqueam have a right to protect their land. After all, the Company would like to set up a fort on the Pacific. We paddle towards the shore as ordered, and when the canoe lands, Fraser asks Stuart, Quesnel and me to get out and walk up the gentle bank towards the longhouses. We do so but as I glance back, I see La Malice is heading off along the beach. Where is he going? I wonder. Seeing no one in the village, we cautiously approach the nearest cedar plank house in the clearing.

I slowly pull aside the fibre mat that covers the door and peer inside. At first I see nothing but darkness, but as my eyes adjust to the gloom, I make out a shape in the corner of the house.

Straining my eyes in the shadows, I make out the shape of an elderly woman. She advances towards me, looking at me solemnly, and I hazard a smile. She lifts her hand in return.

"There is a woman inside," I say, emerging into the sunlight. "She didn't seem hostile."

Suddenly we hear a shot and we see La Malice running back to the canoe waving his pistol.

"What is the matter?" we shout, but La Malice continues running towards the canoe.

"The fool has fired his pistol at someone," Stuart says. "We'll have to show them that we mean them no harm."

Fraser agrees and we return to the canoe to obtain some gifts. As we are searching the canoe, a great shout arises. Warriors, wearing coats of skins and brandishing spears, bows and wicked-looking wooden clubs, burst out of the undergrowth.

"There is no time for peace talks," Fraser shouts.

"Push! Push for your lives!" screams La Malice.

As the warriors advance, Fraser aims his gun. The Musqueam drop to the ground and raise their wooden shields to their heads at the sight of the weapon, but they don't react with terror. Instead, they advance cautiously towards us as we struggle with the canoe. These are clearly confident warriors.

With a mighty heave, the canoe slips free of the mud. We scramble in and plunge our paddles deep into the brown water of the river as spears splash into the water and arrows hiss angrily through the air around us. Several strike the canoe but with a few frantic paddle thrusts, we're safely out of range of the warriors. "What do we do now?" I ask, my terror subsiding.

"Now, Mr. Scott," replies Fraser, "we go home. The tide's rising and that will help us paddle against the current. We will deal with La Malice's stupidity later."

"At least we've followed the Columbia to its mouth," says D'Alaire. "That's a feat no one has done before."

La Certe agrees. "And the Americans haven't arrived yet either."

Fraser casts a knowing glance at me. "Men," he begins solemnly, "you've demonstrated great courage in the face of adversity. Never in the history of the North West Company has a finer group of voyageurs been assembled, nor a nobler task undertaken."

He pauses to let his words sink in. Fraser really is proud of the brigade, I can tell. Lesser men would have deserted weeks ago. "We set out on a mission to follow the Columbia to the sea in the name of King and Company, but through the use of our sextants I began to suspect a day or two ago that this river is not the Columbia. Today when we saw the sea, my fears were confirmed. There is no American fort because we are too far north. This is a different river altogether."

Fraser's revelation stuns the voyageurs. Some of their expressions are blank and unreadable while others are visibly angry. Waccan speaks first, laughing bitterly at the news. "You mean to say that all this time and through all those dangers, we were on the wrong river?"

"Yes, but not intentionally," concedes Fraser. "I truly believed it to be the Columbia."

That does not satisfy La Malice. He bursts out angrily,

"The great Simon Fraser, chasing fame and fortune, risking our necks for nothing!" The worst part of La Malice's taunt is that it's true. If the river was a practical trade route, the journey would have been worth the dangers, but with the rapids and the unfriendly nature of some of its inhabitants, this river will not serve the North West Company or the Empire.

"We'll make it back to Fort St. James," Fraser vows. "And you'll all be well rewarded for your efforts, I promise you."

I see Fraser glance at La Malice and grit his teeth. I wonder what reward he has in mind for the man who set the Musqueam against us.

Gagnier's eyes swivel downriver as several canoes full of armed and chanting warriors rapidly approach. "I hope you're right because if we're to see one penny we'll have to outrun them."

Chapter 36

"SCARE THEM AWAY!" commands Fraser. A warrior stands in the lead Musqueam canoe, closing quickly on us, a long spear held high over his head. At the command, I pull out my pistol and, with a shaking hand, pull the trigger, aiming low. The ball thuds into the canoe by the warrior's leg. The man howls in surprise and drops the spear.

Several others fire as well, shooting into the river. The reports echo across the water, and clouds of acrid smoke cover both us and the Musqueam. When the air clears, we see the warriors have backed off and are slowly drifting away.

"That scared them," says Stuart.

"*Oui*! After them! We've more than enough firepower to

chase them back to their village!" cries Waccan, not one to let a challenge go unanswered.

But Fraser will have none of it. "No! Let them go and keep paddling upstream!" The current is strong, but aided by the rising tide we make good progress. Soon after, the sun sets, and the Musqueam are nowhere in sight, but still we paddle, anxious to put as much distance between us and our pursuers as possible.

The river is wide and illuminated by the full moon that hangs large and silver in the sky. We paddle through the night, and by dawn reach the outskirts of the Sto:lo village where we'd left Little Fellow the day before.

We see our friend and two Sto:lo warriors at the river's edge. Very quickly I can see that something is wrong. Little Fellow's face and arms are bruised and cut, and the men at his side act more like guards than companions.

The two Sto:lo warriors see us coming, yell an alarm and run towards their chief's longhouse. "Flee!" shouts Little Fellow from the bank. "It isn't safe!"

"What happened to you?" Fraser calls back.

"They turned on me. They were about to kill me when the chief changed his mind. Now I am his slave. They also planned to kill you if you returned. They didn't like your taking their canoe. Don't stop for me, keep going and save yourselves."

"We'll not abandon a friend," says Fraser, as the canoe crunches ashore. The explorer hops out and wraps his arm around Little Fellow's shoulders. "We'll leave this place together or not at all."

Before we can push back onto the river, a band of heavily armed men marches up to us. "You live," the chief says, surprise evident in his voice. "I will have my canoe back."

Since the dugout canoe is our only means of escape, Fraser has no plans to return it. At his command, we arrange ourselves defensively around the canoe, our backs to the river, guns and knives drawn.

A Sto:lo warrior raises his spear and as he does Fraser screams at the top of his lungs, waving his hands and shouting in a strange mixture of French, English and gibberish. The man, so brave just a second ago, flees in terror. From a safe distance the chief stares at Fraser, confusion and fear on his face. "Are you Raven?" he asks in awe. "Are you the Trickster?"

With no time to ask what the man means, Fraser pulls Little Fellow into the canoe, we all jump in, and begin hastily paddling away from the village. Before we gain speed, Fraser grabs a blanket and some other goods and throws them onto the shore. "Payment for the loan of the canoe!" he shouts. "We're not thieves. You'll have it back soon enough."

No one follows us. With the strong tide pushing us upriver, the Sto:lo village soon disappears. "Simon, what on earth possessed you to act like that?" asks Stuart. "I almost thought you really were crazy."

"I don't know," Fraser says sheepishly. "I was angry and I

wanted to scare them, I suppose. It just came out. And what was the chief talking about, Little Fellow? Who is this Trickster?"

"The People of the River believe that Raven can transform himself into many forms, even into a man," Little Fellow explains. "Raven is a cunning creature who tricks people into giving him what he wants. I think perhaps the Sto:lo believed you were not a man, but a spirit."

Stuart laughs. "We all know you have a high opinion of yourself, Simon. It seems you've finally met people who agree with you!"

For the second day in a row we travel through the night, Fraser urging us forward with every ounce of energy we possess. I paddle on, shoulders and arms as numb as that night on the *Sylph* when I manned the pumps. It isn't until morning that Fraser orders us ashore to rest, but no sooner does the canoe grind against the gravel beach when La Malice leaps out and pulls his pistol out from his belt.

"Enough!" he screams, aiming the gun at Fraser's head. "I've had enough of this voyage, I've had enough of this cursed river, and I've had enough of you!" Then La Malice issues the challenge that has been building for weeks.

"Who's with me? I know many of you feel the same as I. Now's our chance to leave these damned clerks to their fates. I'm for heading home overland, so think carefully: this could be your last chance to save yourselves."

Chapter 37

SLOWLY WE STEP OUT onto the shore, the voyageurs shuffling uncomfortably together. I know some are already on La Malice's side and that others are seriously considering his proposal. A mutiny is imminent. Quesnel and Stuart flank our commander with pistols drawn. I curse myself that I left my pistol in the canoe, and so with my heart pounding, I pull out my knife and take my place beside Fraser.

Fraser remains calm. "I don't blame you for feeling this way, men. Your lives have been in jeopardy many times, but through it all you've demonstrated more courage and loyalty than I could ever have expected. There's no guarantee we'll make it back alive, but we stand a much better chance if we stick together."

He looks searchingly at each of them, men like Gagnier whom he's known for years. "The Company was built upon friendship, loyalty and courage. Are you willing to toss all that aside? Besides, what chance would you have, travelling alone cross-country in this land? If we go our separate ways we're dead for sure."

Waccan approaches. "Let us men talk alone, Simon. We will come to a decision soon."

"La Malice would put a bullet in my back right now if he could," says Fraser as we walk down the sand bar, away from the voyageurs who begin talking animatedly to one other. "But I'm hoping that Waccan, Gagnier and D'Alaire will convince the others that what I said is true. We wouldn't last a week in this country if we split up. Our strength lies in our numbers."

After ten minutes of what appears to be a heated discussion, the voyageurs signal us to join them. I look at La Malice, trying to guess what the outcome of the conversation has been, but his dark face seems carved from stone: cold, emotionless and unreadable. I listen breathlessly as Waccan speaks on the men's behalf.

"Better the devil you know than the one you don't, *n'est-ce pas*? You have our word that we'll stay together, Monsieur Fraser. Besides," Waccan adds, smiling at me, "if the youngest one among us has the courage to continue, it would look bad on the rest of us if we didn't!"

Judging by the dark expressions on some of their faces the

decision is by no means unanimous. While Fraser is obviously relieved, he needs additional assurances.

"I'm glad we've resolved not to separate during the rest of the voyage," he says, "but I feel we should all take an oath to formalize this decision. If you truly mean what you have said, repeat after me: 'I solemnly swear before almighty God, that I shall sooner perish than forsake in distress any of our crew during the present voyage.'"

The men look at each other hesitantly, then one by one with Waccan in the lead, they remove their hats and repeat the vow solemnly. All that is, except La Malice. Dragged along on a mission that has nearly cost him his life several times over, he has taken all he can, oath or not.

I watch La Malice stretch his left hand slowly behind his back to the pistol tucked in his sash. "Simon, watch out!" I cry. With a curse, La Malice pulls out the pistol, and as he cocks the hammer, I leap forward and slash at his hand.

The shot misses Fraser by several feet. La Malice drops the pistol from his bleeding hand and grabs hold of me instead. "I should have killed you on the cliff, whelp, but I'll make up for that mistake now!"

We struggle, all the while edging closer and closer to the riverbank. La Malice is larger and stronger, and when he reaches hungrily for my knife, I fight back with desperate strength, knowing beyond any doubt what will happen if he gets his hand on it.

La Malice gains the upper hand. His fingers wrap around

mine. He twists my hand and the blade so that they are slowly pushing towards my throat. "Die, boy!" he says, his eyes blazing with rage.

I feel his breath on my face, see through watering eyes the knife edge closer and closer as the larger, heavier man leans into me. I drop quickly to one knee, throw La Malice off balance and then, with all my strength, lower my shoulder and push hard against the voyageur.

La Malice curses, slipping on the wet gravel of the riverbank. He falls backwards, pulling me down on top of him, the knife wedged between our bodies.

"Duncan!" shouts Quesnel, hurrying to pull me off the voyageur. "Are you hurt? It happened so fast I couldn't help!"

Quesnel lifts me up, and I'm horrified to see a dark patch of blood on my shirt. I forget all about La Malice until I hear him cough and see him stagger to his knees, blood flowing from his mouth, staining his black beard crimson.

La Malice struggles to his feet, standing and swaying at the river's edge, a large red stain blossoming across his chest like a flower. He coughs, his lips moving as if he's trying to speak. Then his head slumps and he collapses awkwardly, falling over backwards into the river. I watch in shock as he floats out into the main channel of the river and drifts away in the current.

The blood-stained weapon is still held tightly in my grasp, and I drop it as if it were a poisonous snake. "I didn't mean to kill him! He fell on top of the knife!" My mind races back to

Scotland, to an image of Sir Cecil Hamilton, lying still and bleeding on a Glasgow street. That rash attack forced me from my home and took my sister from me. Who knows what fate awaits me now that I've actually killed a man.

Instead, Fraser embraces me. "You've nothing to be sorry about, lad. You saved my life! The North West Company and I owe you a debt we can never hope to repay." He claps me heartily on the shoulder as one by one the voyageurs shake my trembling hand.

"That's how you deal with traitors, like La Malice," says Waccan, spitting as he mentions the name, handing me back my knife. "I can't believe he would do that."

"*Très courageux*," adds Gagnier with respect. Still numb from what happened, I fall to my knees, face ashen. Quesnel races over to my side and puts his arm around me.

"So what do we do now?" asks Gagnier. "We're hundreds of miles from home, we've no food and are being chased by people who want to kill us."

"Now," replies Fraser, "we light a big fire, and find some clams or berries and whatever else we can. Lord knows what dangers we'll encounter in the morning, but I'd much rather face them on a full belly and in the company of the bravest men I've ever known."

Chapter 38

WE LEAVE THE DUGOUT canoe at Spuzzum, the villagers promising to return it to the Sto:lo. We stay the night then carry on by foot, travelling north.

Several days later, and with my guilt over La Malice starting to fade, I look nervously at the same wooden bridge from which I'd nearly fallen to my death. This time, however, despite several slips and close calls, we all cross safely over the chasm. At dusk we step off the trail, and fall asleep under the stars, too tired even to bother with a fire.

The next morning the mist and rain envelop the path, and our progress is slow, but by the afternoon of the following day we reach Kumsheen. Things are not as they should be at the village where the two rivers meet. "Our people are sick and we've been waiting for your return," says a man as we approach. "The chief says you have powerful medicines. He hopes that you can help us."

Fraser agrees at once. "The Nlaka'pamux have been very generous. We'll repay your kindness as best we can."

A shadow hangs over Kumsheen. The people who'd seemed so healthy just a short while ago now look terrible. Grey skin sags on emaciated frames, and people cough horribly, their chests heaving with wracking gasps.

"Bring the sick to me," Fraser commands. Soon a long line of ill children and their worried mothers forms in front of him. Fraser takes a small glass bottle from his pack and applies a drop of dark liquid to the tongue and forehead of each child. Apparently it is all that remains after most of our medicines were lost when the bale fell into the canyon.

"What's in the bottle?" I whisper.

"Laudanum," says Quesnel. "It can't cure them, but it will dull their pain for a little while. They will be able to rest and perhaps heal. It's the least we can do, Duncan. These people were perfectly healthy before they encountered us. Now they're deathly ill. I don't think that's a coincidence, do you?"

I'm shocked at the suggestion. "Yer not saying we may well be responsible fer this, are ye? None of us were sick when we passed through here."

"Not seriously, no," Quesnel says, "but I'm sure at least one of us had a cold or a cough that we may have unknowingly passed along. These people have never been exposed to our diseases. What may have only been a slight discomfort for us could very well become a death sentence for them."

It makes me feel absolutely terrible that I could be responsible for the misery around me. Then another, disturbing thought occurs. "And when they realize we can't heal them, Jules?"

Quesnel replies grimly. "Then for our sakes we'd better be far from here when that happens."

Chapter 39

"I MUST STAY WITH my people," Little Fellow tells us. "I am worried for them."

Fraser hugs the small man tightly. "I can't thank you enough. Without your help we would never have survived." Over the weeks Little Fellow has become a trusted friend and companion, and we are sad to see him go.

"I'll miss Little Fellow," I say.

"We all will," replies Fraser. "Some call these people 'savages,' and while it's true they live a strange life by our European standards, they're no different in their hearts from any of us. The colour of their skin may be different, but the same strengths and faults we find in Montreal or London are here in the wilds."

We say a sombre farewell to Kumsheen and continue on our way. The weather's awful, the trail's as slippery as ice. To compound our misery, sharp stones slice through the thin leather of our footwear as if it were paper. Every step is torture. To run the risk of infection and go lame in this country could very well mean our death.

We move slowly, stopping frequently to repair our shoes and rest our blistered and bleeding feet, so it's with tremendous relief when, four days later, we reach our cached canoes.

"Things are looking up," says Quesnel. "Our canoes are untouched, and although the current is fast, the river will soon be navigable again. Paddling, even against the current, is a much better option than walking, the shape we are in. We may just get home after all."

Tired and aching, we soon reach Xats'ull. Xlo'sem is there to greet us. "I've looked forward to this day since we parted ways!" he beams.

Fraser heartily agrees. "It's good to be back. We've had many adventures since you left our company. I'd be happy to tell you about them."

If the chief remembers that he'd snuck out of camp in the dead of night without a word of farewell he doesn't bring it up, and neither, diplomatically, does Fraser. "Of course we will hear your story," Xlo'sem replies, "but first we eat. You look terrible and your feet are ready to fall off your legs! The people downriver must not have treated you as well as I did!"

We are indeed a sight. We've all lost so much weight that

our clothes hang in rags around us. We haven't shaved for weeks; even I have the beginnings of a sparse beard on my face. My hair is long and greasy, and I can't remember the last time I bathed. It's a very good thing we aren't making first impressions.

We rest for a few hours then eat the best meal we've had in nearly a month as Fraser recounts our adventures. When he hears about our troubles with the Musqueam and Sto:lo, Xlo'sem leaps up and waves his knife in the air. "I would have ordered my men to war had you been harmed! But something did happen ... You're missing a companion, the one with the black beard and sour face."

"Our only casualty, I'm afraid to say," explains Fraser. "There was an accident downstream and he fell into the river." None of the men say anything. The truth of course is very different, but there's no point in speaking about it here.

We finish our dinner, excuse ourselves and finish setting up camp. "The rain's stopped," I say, staring into the sky. "It looks as if it's going to be hot tomorrow. I'd wager Simon will want to get going as soon as possible."

"I think you're right," replies Quesnel. "Some of the voyageurs want to stay here for a few days, but I know how badly Simon wants to return to Fort St. James. If we don't get back soon it will be too late to send a message to Montreal."

"What do ye think the Company will do?" I ask. "This is a huge setback, isn't it?"

"Perhaps they'll send Simon to search for the headwaters

of the real Columbia," Quesnel says. "Or maybe there's another route altogether that we don't know about. This is wild and unexplored country; I'm sure it has a lot of surprises left in store for us."

The next morning there is indeed a surprise waiting for us, but it doesn't come from the land. Despite Quesnel's thoughts to the contrary, Fraser tells us that he's agreed to stay with the Secwepemc for two more days.

"It's a good idea," says Quesnel. "This is the first true day of rest we've enjoyed in nearly six weeks. It will do us and our feet a world of good. Besides, we dodged one mutiny; I don't think Simon wants to encourage another one."

In all, we spend three days swimming in a quiet backwater of the river and lounging in the hot sun. We could have stayed for weeks, but despite the protestations of the chief to remain, Fraser is adamant we leave.

Xlo'sem bids us an emotional goodbye, making Fraser promise to return as soon as he can. The people give us food and an ample supply of leather moccasins, along with bear grease to treat the sores on our feet. With the chief and the rest of the Secwepemc people waving from the shore, we push off into the river and paddle north.

We travel steadily upstream for several days, and our food situation greatly improves when, to the delight of all, Waccan finally shoots a deer. We eat fresh venison and are surprised to discover that our salmon caches are intact as well. Remarkably, some of the fish is still edible.

"We passed Mackenzie's trail yesterday. One more patch of

rough water and it's clear sailing to Fort George," says Fraser.

"And about time, Simon," says Stuart. "Your river may never see another North West Company canoe, but that doesn't take away from what we've done. And who knows, perhaps it will prove useful after all. If that day comes, people will have the men of the North West Company to thank for it."

"I'm not concerned about the gratitude of future generations," says Waccan, chewing on a dry piece of salmon the colour of paper. "I never thought I'd say it but I just want to get back to Fort St. James."

"Then we'd best get you back soon," promises Fraser. "Ten days from now, this trip will be over and consigned to the history books."

It's a warm night. The campfire crackles and pops as I watch the embers spiral up into the sky. There have been times on the journey I felt certain that I'd die and never see Liverpool or any other place again. But I have to admit that travelling the river has been the most remarkable experience of my life.

I remember Louise, and my hand travels absently to the medicine bag resting against my chest. It's almost full now. Inside the leather pouch are treasures, including a pebble from the shores of Stuart's Lake, a piece of wood from the hanging bridge that almost cost me my life, a shell from the muddy banks of the estuary, and a Musqueam arrowhead I'd dug out of the canoe. These are my memories of an amazing adventure. I'm anxious to show them to Louise, and tell her the stories that accompany them.

"Two years," I say to myself. "I wonder what else can possibly happen before I get home."

But there's no home anymore for me. Just Libby, somewhere back in England, and even if by some miracle I return, would I even recognize my sister? Probably, but she was little more than a girl at our parting in Liverpool. Now she would be a woman. Which makes me, I realize with a start, a man.

I run my hand over my face, feeling my moustache and thin beard. And would she know me? I hope to find out soon. I've more than completed the mission I was sent on by Mc-Gillivray, but have no idea when, or even if, Fraser plans to send me back to Montreal.

On the afternoon of the sixth of August, two months and a week after we left it, Fort George appears ahead in the distance. Several figures emerge from the small log cabin, waving and shouting excitedly as the canoes slide gently ashore. "You're alive! I can't believe it!" cries Hugh Faries. "I gave you up for dead weeks ago!"

"You should know it takes more than a little voyage to the sea to kill a Nor'Wester, Mr. Faries," replies Fraser.

"So the Columbia does reach the Pacific just as you thought it would!" Faries is ecstatic at the news.

Fraser shakes his head. "The Columbia does indeed reach the sea but this river, I'm afraid, is not the Columbia. Now put the kettle on and make us some tea, Hugh. I have quite a story to tell you."

Chapter 40

DAYS LATER, BACK at Fort St. James, I net and smoke salmon, chop firewood, and for the second time since arriving in New Caledonia, prepare the fort for the impending arrival of winter.

I've hardly seen the explorer in the two weeks we've been back, and as desperate as I am to go home to England, I haven't had the opportunity to talk to him about leaving — until he summons me one late August afternoon.

"I wanted to thank you again for saving my life," says Fraser when I step into his cabin. "La Malice was a dangerous man. You could have been killed stepping in like that. It was a rash and impulsive act, but I'm very glad you did it."

"I've a tendency to act quickly and worry about the consequences later," I say. "At least I did when I was younger. My sister used to spend a great deal of time getting me out of trouble."

"It's your sister I wanted to talk to you about," he says. I'm taken aback. Although I've spoken briefly of my family to Jules Quesnel, nobody except for Louise has heard the full story.

"No need to be surprised," Fraser reassures me. "Mr. Quesnel mentioned to me the other day that you have a sister in England who couldn't come with you to Montreal."

"Aye, that's true," I say warily, not knowing what else Fraser may know.

"Quesnel also told me that you want to return to England to see her. Is that correct?"

"Aye, but I wouldn't want to disappoint Mr. McGillivray. The North West Company has been kind to me, and I'm in yer debt."

Fraser hands me a thin book wrapped in an oilskin. "This is my account of our journey. I'm sending you to Montreal to deliver it to McGillivray personally. Both the Company and Empire need the information, disappointing though it is. Gagnier will take you to Fort Dunvegan with orders for Luc Lapointe to accompany you to Montreal."

"Aye, Sir," I reply, as a huge smile creases my face.

"Feel free to tell Lapointe about our adventure, and Callum Mackay as well when you reach Fort William, but say nothing to anyone else; the world doesn't need to hear about my failure in the West quite yet."

Fraser shakes my hand heartily. "I'm going to miss you, Duncan. It would be an honour to travel with you again."

"Thank ye, Sir," I say, struggling to control my emotions. "I'll never forget ye — or this place."

"I hope not," Fraser says. "After all, you've become part of its history."

Gagnier and I leave for Fort Dunvegan the next morning. It's far too late in the year to make it to Montreal before the rivers freeze, but with luck we'll get as far as Red River. Despite my desire to find Libby, my heart races at the prospect of spending time with the Métis.

We complete the long portage, return to Fort Misery, then make our way back to the Peace River. As we paddle east, my mind fills with plans. I'll winter with Louise and then in the spring the two of us will leave together for England, find Libby and return to Red River. It's a good plan, one that occupies my mind constantly as we push east through the mountains.

We travel through the mountains and arrive at Fort Dunvegan ten days later. I'm thrilled to see Luc Lapointe, and despite being tired from the trip, we leave for Red River the very next day. Winter's coming and speed is of the essence.

The days are still bright and warm, but Lapointe packs his heaviest winter clothes, along with an extra coat for me.

"We'll be grateful for these before our trip is through," he prophesies. "It's a little late in the year to be making this voyage, but the Company needs to hear this news. I can't imagine how Simon feels. He's put a lot of stock in the river. His reputation is going to take a blow."

We travel quickly as the days shorten and the weeks pass by. Though morning frost soon lies thick on the ground, and the quiet back-eddies and oxbows of the rivers freeze, the main streams still run free. By late October, Red River is only a few days away.

On the day we arrive, the first snowfall of winter hits hard, and we're greatly relieved to see the Métis village. "*Mes amis*! Welcome!" cries the voice of Louis Desjarlais through the midday flurries. "Come and warm yourselves by the fire. It's too cold to be on the water today!"

The heat from Desjarlais' hearth sweeps over us as we are escorted into his cabin, but a strange air hangs over the place. "Louis, are ye all right?" I ask as we enter the building.

The large Métis man breaks into tears. "It's Louise. Last winter she fell sick. At first I thought it was just a cold but she didn't get better. Then she caught a terrible fever. No matter what we did, she lay in bed, growing weaker and weaker until she died in my arms."

I feel my legs buckle under me and would have fallen to the floor had Desjarlais not wrapped me tightly in a giant hug.

"Her grave is out on the prairie she loved so much, Duncan. I'll take you to it if you like."

Louise rests on the same hill where we'd spotted the buffalo. A small cross sits above her grave, the hard prairie wind pushing the falling snow up against the base of the wooden marker. "Take all the time you need," says Desjarlais before he and Lapointe walk back to the settlement.

I stand alone in front of the rough wooden cross, struggling to find the words. When I finally speak, I talk to Louise as if she were still alive. "I vowed to see ye again, Louise, but I'm afraid I can't keep that promise. A dinnae ken if ye can hear me, but I would still like to tell ye about my adventures."

I take the medicine bag from my neck and talk for more than an hour, recounting everything that's happened since leaving Red River. When I finish my story, a wave of grief sweeps over me, as powerful as when my parents died.

I fall to my knees and cry, weeping for my mother and father, lost in a Glasgow fire. I cry for Francis and for the young boy I met in Liverpool, both dead in the dark Atlantic.

I cry for the sick children of Kumsheen and I cry for Libby, alone somewhere in England. I cry for Louise as well. I barely knew her but felt a connection to her as deep and powerful as any I've experienced in my short life. "I will never forget ye, Louise," I say, finally getting to my feet. I brush the snow off my legs, and then, without looking back, I walk towards the Métis village.

When I return to the cabin, Desjarlais is waiting for me. He gives me a large tanned buffalo robe, thick with hair. "Louise made this for you before she fell sick," he says. The robe's decorated with beads and porcupine quills. Sewn into the skin is a needlework portrait of a man and woman riding on a large black horse against a prairie backdrop. Louise has captured perfectly our one day on the prairies together.

"It's beautiful," I tell him.

"A winter-kill buffalo robe will keep you warm on even the coldest nights," says Desjarlais. "I knew my girl had talent but I've never seen the likes of this robe before."

I love the robe but I know too well the pain of losing a family member, so if I can give Desjarlais something to remember his daughter I'm glad to do it. "Would ye like to have it, Louis?" I ask.

Desjarlais is aghast. "Don't even suggest it! This is a gift of love; you must keep it."

"This fell out of the robe," says Lapointe handing me a thin piece of fabric he's picked up from the floor.

It's as if I see a ghost. "The embroidery. My mother made it in Scotland," I say softly. "I gave it to Louise before I left."

"And she must have wanted you to have it back," says Desjarlais.

Our host excuses himself for the night. "What do you think?" asks Lapointe when we're alone. "Do we stay here for the winter or try for Fort William?"

Without Louise there's nothing to hold me at Red River anymore. "I just want to go," I say.

"*Bien*, I agree. It's cold but the rivers are still navigable. Besides, the news you carry is too important to sit on here.

We'll say our goodbyes and leave first thing in the morning. Who knows? With that robe, a bit of luck and a prayer or two to Sainte Anne and *La Vieille*, we just might make it to Fort William before we freeze to death."

Chapter 41

THE GREEN-NEEDLED evergreens on the hills are washed out and faded, and the birch and cottonwood trees, stripped of their leaves, rise ghost-like above the icy banks of the river. The wind is constant, and we exist in a constant state of cold. Lapointe and I say little as we paddle, and during the long bitter nights, we huddle for warmth under our canoe, gratefully wrapped up together in Louise's robe. There is no doubt that without it, the cold would claim us both.

By the middle of December we reach the vast grey mass of Lake Superior. "Thank goodness," says Lapointe. "Another two days, three at the most and we'd have been in real trouble. It's a miracle we made it this far."

"Maybe those prayers we sent to Sainte Anne de Bellevue worked after all," I say.

"I hope Sainte Anne and *La Vieille* are still looking out for us, Duncan," says Lapointe. "We still have to travel one hundred miles on the roughest lake in the world. It's going to take both of their help to get us to Fort William alive."

We paddle safely for several days until a storm blows in. The wind picks up so we head to shore, build a fire and huddle round the flames as the flakes fall, slowly at first but with ever-increasing size and frequency until there's nothing but a swirling tornado of white. "This is going to be bad, isn't it?" I say.

"*Oui*," replies Lapointe. "We need to get under the canoe and out of the storm's way; God only knows when it will end."

For twelve hours the snow falls. The wind howls around us, and despite the shelter of the birchbark canoe and the thick buffalo robe, I feel as if I'm turning to ice myself. When the storm finally subsides, we climb out from under the canoe, brush ourselves off and paddle out onto the black water.

"I'm hoping we reach the fort tonight," says Lapointe, his beard frosted from his breath and the icy water that splashes over the gunwales. "The temperature's dropping, and I'd rather not spend another night in the open if I can help it. The ice inside the canoe is very dangerous; it shifts our balance and we could tip over or even break in two with just the slightest wave."

"How cold do ye think it is?" I ask, the frigid air burning my lungs.

"Cold enough to kill the both of us in a matter of seconds if we fall in, so stop talking and save your energy for paddling; we'll have plenty of opportunity to gossip when we reach Fort William. Mackay and the others will want to know what could possibly be so important as to make this insane trip!"

The shadowy bulk of Fort William finally appears through the blowing snow. "Travellers!" the lookout cries in disbelief when we beach the canoe. Callum Mackay hears the shout and runs to the lakefront, his great red beard waving like a flag. It's almost unprecedented for a canoe to arrive this late in the season, and never from the west.

"My God!" he exclaims as we stagger onto the shore. "The pair o' ye must be mad! It's a miracle the wolves aren't chewing on yer frozen corpses as we speak! What are ye doing back here this time o' year?"

Mackay walks us into the fort. Soon we sit wrapped in blankets, steaming cups of tea in our hands. In the great stone fireplace, the flames soar high, and warmth floods into the Great Hall. "Now what in blazes can be so important ye'd risk travelling in winter?" asks Mackay.

I pass him Fraser's journal, my frozen fingers finally warming up. "This is," I say.

Mackay reads in silence for the better part of fifteen minutes as he digests the contents of the report carefully. "Och!

That is news, isn't it? His lairdship won't be happy fer sure. And that damned La Malice! I always knew he'd do something, but it's an evil day when one o' yer own turns to treason. Guid fer ye, though, lad! I knew ye had courage when I first laid eyes on ye."

"I wouldn't call it bravery," I say. "I was terrified."

Mackay slaps me on the back. "Son, courage is being scared half to death but doing the right thing anyway. The two of ye will winter here, of course, and leave fer Montreal as soon as the ice allows it to give his lairdship the message. It won't be a holiday, though. There's plenty o' work I can find to keep ye busy, but tonight ye'll have a hot meal and rest in a warm bed instead o' sleeping underneath a canoe!"

Chapter 42

"'TIS A WEE BIT early fer a full brigade to travel east," says Mackay as the watery March sun peeks through Fort William's ice-frosted windows. It has been a long winter and Mackay has kept his word. We have been most busy doing chores around the fort.

"However, the two of ye should be able to pick yer way to Montreal by now. There's still snow on the ground, but ye'll leave tomorrow anyway. McGillivray's waited long enough fer this news."

With little ceremony save a crushing bear hug, we slip away from the wharf, heading east towards Lake Huron. In many places the rivers are still frozen and snow continues to fall well into April, but each day is warmer than the last, and we make good time. "La Grande Chaudière!" exclaims Lapointe more than a month after leaving Fort William, as a distant thunder rises on the early May wind. "We'll be in Montreal in just a couple of days."

We quickly portage the waterfall, stop briefly to give thanks at Sainte Anne de Bellevue, and then continue almost immediately, excitement building with each paddle stroke. When a dour stone building comes into view on the banks of the river, I almost cry with joy.

With Fraser's report burning in my vest, there's little time for visiting at Lachine, so we haul the canoe onto the shore and hurry down the wagon path to Montreal.

Without bothering to knock, Lapointe throws open Henry Mackenzie's office door. Mackenzie stands up from his desk, the same desk he'd been working at when I first saw him. "Luc Lapointe, this is a surprise! And who is this voyageur?" he adds, staring blankly at me. "I don't recognize him."

"Sir, I'm Duncan Scott. Ye hired me, remember? Mr. McGillivray sent me west to New Caledonia."

Mackenzie slumps back into his chair, dumbfounded. "My goodness! You went out a boy and have come back a man!"

"We've urgent news from Fraser," says Lapointe. "Where can we find Mr. McGillivray?"

"What news?" A deep voice asks from the doorway. "Tell me quickly: did you make it to the Pacific? Did you beat the Americans?"

I hand over the confidential report and the letter from Fraser that I've carried since last summer. "Sir, we did reach the mouth of the river, but we didn't find any Americans. The river isn't the Columbia, ye see."

"Damnation!" McGillivray frowns. "That is bad news! But this new river?" he asks hopefully. "Do we have a new trade route to the Pacific?"

"I'm afraid not. The river is far too wild fer commerce, and some of the people we encountered were less than hospitable. Read the report, Sir," I say. "It sounds fantastic but I was there, and I can assure ye that every word in it is true."

Chapter 43

"YOU'VE HAD QUITE the adventure, young man," McGillivray says when I'm summoned to his office the following morning. "Simon seems to think you saved his life and, indeed, the very expedition. He calls you a hero for taking care of that traitor, La Malice."

I blush. "I wouldn't say that, Sir."

"Well Fraser does, so I do as well. Simon also says you've some pressing business to attend to in England, but he doesn't go into detail. What's that all about?" McGillivray asks.

"My sister, Sir," I say with surprise. "We were separated in Liverpool. She didn't make the ship. I want very much to go back and find her."

"Ah yes," he replies. "She was mentioned on that poster as well, wasn't she? I'm sorry I used your misfortune against you, young man, but I'm sure you can understand now the importance of the message. I needed someone I could trust to deliver it and that was you."

McGillivray reaches into a desk drawer and removes my wanted poster, now yellowing with age. He stands up, walks to the fireplace in the corner of the room and tosses the paper into the flames. I watch silently as it catches fire and is quickly consumed.

"And now you need to go home. I understand completely. I would love for you to stay on with us, but you've certainly earned a break from the wilds. Go back to England with my blessing. No doubt it's safe for you now, but would you mind doing one last job for me before you go? There's another message I need delivered."

I shudder at the request. The last letter I carried for William McGillivray took two years of my life to deliver.

"Anything, Mr. McGillivray. The Company's been very guid to me," I say, trying to keep my composure.

McGillivray hands me a letter sealed with a red wax stamp. "Don't worry," he smiles. "You're not going back to the Pacific. I need to send word to the Colonial Office in London. There's more at stake in New Caledonia than just our business. The Empire has a vested interest in the territory, and the proper authorities will need to know about Fraser's journey and our mistake about the Columbia. Can you do this?"

"Aye!" I reply gladly. This is one letter I won't mind at all delivering.

McGillivray reaches into his desk drawer and withdraws a handful of silver coins. "There's also the matter of your pay. I've taken the liberty of obtaining the money you gave Henry for safe keeping before you headed west. I've also given you your wages — plus a little bonus for courage and exceptional service to the Company."

I can scarcely believe the small fortune on the desk belongs to me. "Thank ye, Sir," I say gratefully. The money is certainly more than enough to get me home.

McGillivray gives me an additional large gold coin and a folded piece of paper. "The paper identifies you as a North West Company messenger, named McTavish," McGillivray says. "Just in case anyone is still looking for Duncan Scott. The gold is for your fare to England. Costs have gone up since you've been out west."

"Ye're going to pay my passage to England?" The day is getting better and better.

"You're my envoy, lad!" smiles McGillivray. "Besides, with the war in Europe, passage on commercial ships has become almost impossible to find. What few berths there are would cost more than you have."

"What war?" I ask. "With who?"

"The French of course," he says. "Who else?"

It's a good point. England has been at war with the French since I was a small child. "So how am I to travel then?"

"A cargo ship under contract with the Navy leaves for Liverpool tomorrow. I've made arrangements with her captain. Technically, you're no longer a civilian. You are a representative of the Crown, travelling on a diplomatic mission. Be there at first light, the ship sails at dawn."

I'm overwhelmed at the news. "Thank ye, Sir, I promise I won't let ye down."

"You told me that when I first hired you," McGillivray says. "I believed it then, and I believe it now. Go to the Colonial Office in London. Tell them that you're an emissary from Montreal and that you carry confidential news critical to the Empire. It's to be given by you personally to the secretary of state for the colonies. No one else is to have it."

McGillivray shakes my hand warmly. "Good luck, Duncan Scott, and safe travelling. Should you ever return to Montreal there will always be a position waiting for you. After all — once a Nor'Wester always a Nor'Wester!"

Chapter 44

THE *BALTASARA* IS BOUND for Liverpool, carrying white pine and oak for warship construction. Its captain studies me quizzically as I board, telling me that even with the letter of introduction from McGillivray, I seem far too young to be a diplomatic courier.

"The trip will take the better part of two months through some of the roughest water on earth, lad. If the spring storms aren't enough, Boney's entire Atlantic fleet is out there waiting to sink us."

The wind freshens as he speaks, lines snapping sharply to attention in the breeze. "Are you sure you don't want to stay in Montreal?" he asks. "Speak now: we're leaving any moment, and once we clear the dock there's no guarantee we'll ever see home again."

But home isn't Montreal. Home is Libby. She's out there somewhere, and I will find her no matter how long it takes.

"Sometimes, Captain," I say, "fate makes other plans fer us. Show me where I can stow my things. I'm ready to go."

AUTHOR'S NOTE

The Nor'Wester is a work of fiction. While Simon Fraser and the men
of the North West Company did embark on a journey to the Pacific in
1808, there is nothing in the historical record to indicate they did so as
an official response to the journey of Lewis and Clark.

Simon Fraser, John Stuart, Jules Quesnel, Hugh Faries and the
voyageurs that Duncan meets in Fort St. James are real, including the
unpleasant La Malice, although his hatred of Duncan and his fate as
described in this book are fiction.

Additionally, while there is no evidence to show that Duyunun accompanied Fraser down the river, he, Chief Kwah, and the other Indigenous people described in this book, including Little Fellow, were
real historical figures. The journey is heavily based on Fraser's own
journal, and some of Fraser's dialogue is taken from the very words he

used in his own account. The village of Chunlac is a real place, and the massacre described in the book is an historical event that occurred around the year 1750.

There was a migrant ship called the *Sylph* that travelled the Atlantic Ocean from Liverpool to Quebec in the early years of the 19th century, and although Tom and Francis are fictional characters, the description of the Atlantic crossing is based on first-hand accounts from both crew members and passengers who made the hazardous journey.

John Davis, Henry Mackenzie, Luc Lapointe, Callum Mackay and Louis and Louise Desjarlais are all fictional. William McGillivray was the head of the North West Company, and the descriptions of the North West Company headquarters, Lachine, Fort William and Fort St. James are historically accurate.

A word on the names of the Indigenous peoples used in this account: there was a conscious effort to respect and use the names preferred by the Native peoples themselves, instead of the names ascribed to them by Fraser and others, including "Indian." For example, the Secwepemc (pronounced *She-whep-m*) were called the "Atnah" by Fraser and have, at various other times in history, been given other names. Nlaka'pamux is pronounced *Ing-khla-kap-muh*; in Fraser's journal they were called the "Hacamaugh."

Two books in particular were invaluable to the creation of this story. The first is Stephen Hume's *Simon Fraser: In Search of Modern British Columbia* (Harbour Publishing, 2008). The second is W. Kaye Lamb's edition of *The Letters and Journals of Simon Fraser, 1806–1808* (reprinted by Dundurn Press, 2007). A third book, Bruce Hutchinson's *The Fraser* (Irwin Publishing, 1982), is also an important resource for those seeking more information about this fascinating period of early British Columbia history.

ABOUT THE AUTHOR

David Starr is a prize-winning author of three previous books. In *Bombs to Books*, he chronicled the stories of refugee children and their families coming to B.C. *Golden Goal* is a young adult soccer-themed book for reluctant readers. *The Insider's Guide to K–12 Education in B.C.* is a resource guide for parents about the B.C. school system. David grew up in Fort St. James, a town that plays a large role in *The Nor'Wester*. He now lives in greater Vancouver with his wife, four children and a dog named Buster. He combines the roles of high school principal and author.